BLACK SUITS FROM
OUTER SPACE

OTHER YEARLING BOOKS YOU WILL ENJOY:

BLACK SUITS FROM OUTER SPACE

◆ Gene DeWeese ◆

A Yearling Book

Published by
Dell Publishing
a division of
Bantam Doubleday Dell Publishing Group, Inc.
666 Fifth Avenue
New York, New York 10103

ISBN: 0-440-40196-8

Reprinted by arrangement with The Putnam & Grosset Group

Printed in the United States of America

July 1989

10 9 8 7 6 5 4 3 2

FOR PAULETTE MINARÉ,

*with thanks for the kind words you've
had for some of my earlier efforts, and in
hopes that you'll enjoy this and
future ones just as much.*

CONTENTS

"As Long As Your Whole Life Doesn't Turn Out to Be a Squashed Bottle Cap, You're Okay."

I was almost twelve when I met my first monster from outer space.

Or maybe I should say the first one I *knew* about. Actually, for all I know, the whole world could be up to its armpits in aliens every other weekend, and if East Gradwohl's any example, it probably *is*, and not just on weekends.

The thing is, when their gadgets are all working right, they look just like us, more or less. But when things go wrong, like they did last spring around here, and their computers' wheels start falling off—well, that's another kettle of carp altogether.

My name, by the way, is Calvin Willeford, which, I hate to admit, sort of fits me. It's not so much the way I look, although that's part of it. For one thing I'm quite a bit skinnier than I consider absolutely necessary, especially for someone who lives on double rations of cheeseburgers, pizzas, and extra-thick chocolate shakes. Then there are the glasses. You'd never see a Jason or a Derek wearing glasses, except maybe contact lenses, even if he needed them, but on a Calvin, they fit right in.

But the main thing is, I've been known to be a bit on the klutzy side now and then. You know the sort of thing. You're pedaling along on your bike and you see a quarter in the gutter, and you stop and go back, but when you try to pick it up, you're still straddling your bike, so you lean over too far and everything in your shirt pocket falls in the gutter, and on top of that, the quarter turns out to be a squashed bottle cap.

But I guess things could be worse. At least according to my best friend, Kathy Entsminger, they could be. Like she said once after she'd watched me trying to clean the gutter goop off a brand new package of Spearmint before stuffing it back in my pocket, "As long as your whole life doesn't turn out to be a squashed bottle cap, you're okay."

Which may give you some idea what being best friends with someone like Kathy is like. I mean, I hardly ever think of lines like that, even though I wish I did now and then. Kathy says I'm too logical, and logic isn't a whole lot of help when it comes to seeing a connection between life and a bottle cap, squashed or otherwise. Or a cream cheese sandwich, which was another of her more memorable comparisons.

She's also the only girl I know who has a papier mâché boulder in her folks' garage, which I suppose I should mention, considering the way things turned out. She made it for the school play last year in the fifth grade, in case you're wondering.

But she's right about me being logical. For one thing, Dad would probably disown me if I wasn't. He's an engineer at Harding Microelectronics out on the bypass east of town. He designs computer chips for everything from talking refrigerators to space probes, and if something can't be programed into one of his chips or plugged into an equation somewhere, he has trouble believing it really exists.

Or so he says. There are times when I have my doubts, though. After all, he and Mom have gotten along pretty well for almost fifteen years, and she tends to be a little on the warped side now and then, at least by his standards. Nothing really off the wall, like believing in astrology or anything totally flaky like that, but she does go by "intuition" a lot, especially when it comes to selling houses, which she does for Carbuncle Realty two or three days a week. (Actually, it's Car*michael*, but my tongue got twisted one day, and it's been Carbuncle ever since, at least to Mom. And Kathy, of course.)

Mom used to be an English teacher over in Cranston, but that was, as she says whenever anyone asks her, "before the teacher shortage turned into a teacher surplus." She also has red hair that's curly enough to be the envy of straight-haired types like Kathy, or at least that's what Kathy says. I have a crew cut myself, which is, to quote Dad, "the only logical haircut to have." I mean, who needs to waste all that time with a comb and then have it all fall down in your face anyway?

But about Mom and her intuition. "I knew what that man wanted the second he came in the door," she'll say, telling all of us about her latest sale. "He just *looked* like a north side split level, no matter what he *said* he wanted."

The weird thing about it—and all that keeps Dad from making more cracks than he does—is that sometimes it works. She does have a pretty good track record at Carbuncle, along with a couple of those gold-plated salesperson-of-the-month plaques to prove it, not to mention the commissions.

With me, though—and with Dad, I guess—it's hard *not* to be logical. I mean, it would be like turning off part of your head.

Like when I saw *E.T.*, I kept thinking, why didn't the little dummy just fly back to the ship right at the start? I mean, when the cops were after them an hour later, he was slinging those kids and their bicycles through the air like a bunch of two-wheeled Frisbees, so why couldn't he have slung *himself* through the air right after the opening credits and gotten back to the ship in plenty of time to keep from getting left behind?

"That's easy," Kathy had said. "Then the movie would've been only five minutes long."

Which was, I guess, true enough, but it's just another example of where Kathy's at. I may be too logical most of the time, but she's got the neighborhood market on sarcasm cornered. Except for maybe a little that's rubbed off on me. I mean, you can't be around her and her cracks very long without starting to wish you could think of some of them yourself. Or at least that's how it worked with me. In fact, that's probably one of the reasons we get along as well as we do. I can't help but give her a lot of straight lines, and her cracks are usually the sort of thing I wish I'd thought of myself. I don't even mind when she calls me Mr. Spock. In fact, I take it as a sort of a compliment.

By the way, I wouldn't want anyone to think I didn't like E.T. Sure, the logic was full of holes, but it was fun. Even Dad liked it, but I think he had his own reasons. He figured it might be good for Harding's business, and I sort of see what he means. Like I said, Harding makes computer chips for space probes now and then, and people are all the time asking why we want to spend all that money throwing stuff into outer space. Well, maybe E.T. made a few people realize that just because you're from outer space, you don't have to be some kind of slime monster or maybe a Klingon, like in all the old movies and TV shows. I mean, if all we're going to find out there is a slime monster or a Klingon, I don't think I'd want to do much looking either.

As for what we're really going to find . . .

But maybe I should start at the beginning. Kathy says that's always a good idea, "which anyone as logical as you are should already know."

For me, anyway, it started when that funny-looking cat followed me home. At least I think it followed me home. I'd seen it a few times around school—the Vernon J. Dalhart Middle School, about six blocks from where I live—but never around the house.

If it was the same cat, that is. The trouble was, it was the plainest-looking cat you ever saw, sort of grayish-black all over, without any markings at all, not even on its feet or stomach. Sort of generic, like those extra-plain boxes in the generic corner of the supermarket, where a box of soap flakes looks exactly like a box of dog food except for the words SOAP FLAKES or DOG FOOD printed across the front. Well, this was the sort of cat that maybe needed a little sign hanging around its neck saying CAT.

Anyway, this one afternoon in late May, just a couple of weeks before school was ready to let out for the summer, I came home the way I usually do and unlocked the front door. Dad was still at work, and this was one of Mom's Carbuncle days, so I had the place to myself for at least another hour.

Except for Hulk, that is. Hulk is my cat, and at a tiger-striped twenty pounds, he's about as ungeneric as you can get.

But like I started to say, I had just unlocked the door when this generic-looking cat showed up again. Not only showed up but zipped right past me and through the door.

Needless to say, Hulk—who answers the door like a meowing burglar alarm—wasn't any too thrilled about this invasion of his territory. Or maybe he just wanted to play. Sometimes it's hard to tell with him. But whatever Hulk had in mind, Generic must've figured that this hairy Sherman tank bearing down on him meant business.

Anyway, Generic and I hadn't been in the house more than a couple of seconds when a lot of hissing and spitting broke out. Now I know better than to try to break up a cat fight by grabbing one of the cats. I mean, I like cats

16

and I get along with most of them and all that, but I'm not totally dumb. Having my fingers shredded up to my elbows is not on my list of things to try out just in case I might like them.

It took me about ten seconds to make it to the kitchen, grab a glass from the dish drainer, slop some water in it, and gallop back to the front hall. By the time I got there, things had gone from simple hissing to growling and yowling, and Hulk was in the process of pulling his favorite trick, which is to say, leaping about two feet straight up and coming down with a splat on top of who-ever he's tangling with. Generic, of course, didn't really care for this development, and things got even noisier, fast.

Finally, I got around to heaving the water, at which point Hulk did another straight-up leap, only this time he came down facing me and looking confused, not to men-tion soggy. But at least he wasn't growling anymore, or chewing on Generic.

As for Generic, he didn't do *anything* for a second or two, not even look wet.

But then he made up for lost time.

He gave off a little spark, like the static electricity spark you get when you shuffle your feet on a thick rug. And then he disappeared.

Literally. *He disappeared.*

But what's worse, he reappeared, only he didn't look like a generic cat anymore. Or like any kind of cat at all. He just looked like a blur, a really ugly little blur, sort of like the Tasmanian Devil in those Bugs Bunny cartoons on Saturday morning.

And before I could convince myself the blur was real, let alone get a good look at it and see just how ugly it *really* was, it was out the door and scuttling frantically across the yard and through the bushes.

And that, though I didn't know it at the time, was how I met—and doused—my first visitor from outer space.

· 2 ·

"What Would Mr. Spock Do in a Situation Like This?"

I t wasn't until the blur was out of sight altogether that I started wondering how it had gotten through the screen door. Whatever the thing was, it hadn't been big enough to reach the latch, but that hadn't stopped it.

Probably, I told myself, the latch hadn't caught when I came in. Hulk had gotten out that way more than once. The only trouble was, Dad had fixed the door last month, and Hulk hadn't gotten out since. But it was probably going bad again, that was all. I mean, what other logical explanation could there be?

Meanwhile, Hulk had quit looking around like he was waiting for another flood to fall out of the sky. Instead, he was walking slowly away, pausing and shaking himself every step or two and then holding his feet a couple of inches off the floor one at a time and shaking *them*, like he'd stepped in something he didn't like.

I got a handful of paper towels from the kitchen and started wiping things up, starting with Hulk, who wasn't any happier about that than he had been about the original dousing. Still, after only a couple of meows of protest, he at least wasn't dripping anymore, and he settled down under the coffee table for some serious washing on his own.

Then, still on my hands and knees, I started dabbing at the rug with some wadded-up paper towels, figuring that if I soaked up enough of the water, it would all be dry by the time Mom got home, and nobody would know the difference. But then I felt this lump under the paper towel, right where Generic and Hulk had been going at it. I made a face, figuring it might be one of Hulk's hairballs—or worse—and scooped it up carefully with the wad of wet towels.

But when I turned the wad over, it wasn't a hairball. For a second, I thought it might be some toy Hulk had lost, although those usually show up under the furniture, not out in the open.

But it wasn't a toy, either.

It was a ring.

It didn't look much like any ring I'd ever seen, though, certainly nothing like Dad's old college Engineering Society ring or Mom's little opal. Like Generic, it was sort of grayish-black, and on one side, instead of a setting, there was a big, rectangular lump. In a way, the whole thing looked sort of like a wrist watch, only it was all solid metal with no dial or buttons or windows or anything,

20

and it was only big enough to fit around your thumb, not your wrist.

Lifting up my glasses to look under them, I held the thing up close. Now normally, since I'm so nearsighted, holding something a half inch or so past the end of my nose is sort of like looking at it through a magnifying glass, but this time it didn't work. It just kept looking blurry, like I was looking at a picture that-was out of focus.

The trouble was, my fingers, the fingers I was holding the ring with, were as clear as anything. I could see every little twist and turn in my fingerprints, but the ring, especially the lump, just stayed fuzzy-looking.

Believe it or not, I found myself wondering what Mr. Spock would do in a situation like this, but it didn't do much good. He would use his Tricorder or maybe the whole *Enterprise* computer to analyze the ring, and then he'd scan the neighborhood, or maybe the whole planet, for lifeform readings. Unfortunately, I didn't have so much as a microscope, let alone a Tricorder.

But it didn't make any difference. Before I had time to really *think* about it, I put the ring on. Don't ask me why, I just did. It was the kind of thing that if I'd seen anyone in a movie do it, I'd have been thinking how incredibly dumb it was.

In fact, I *did* think it was pretty dumb, but that's about all I had time for, one quick, "That was really dumb, Calvin Willeford!" As for the ring, it just dangled on my finger, so loose I could've whirled it around like a miniature hula hoop.

But then—well, all I know is, one second the ring was

so big it would've fallen off *Dad's* finger, let alone mine, and the next second it fit me perfectly.

And it wasn't blurred anymore.

The whole thing was like one of those optical illusions, you know the kind. There's a set of stair steps or the outline of a box or something like that, and you can stare right at them and all of a sudden they look like they've flipped upside down or inside out or whatever. Nothing has moved, obviously, since the picture's nothing but a bunch of lines printed on a piece of paper, but all of a sudden it looks different.

Well, that's what this was like, only it was in three dimensions. And, what was worse, it was on my finger.

I jerked my hand back like a spider'd just dropped on it, and I grabbed the ring with my right hand and started to yank it off, but it wouldn't go past my knuckle, which I *knew* was impossible, but it wouldn't budge anyway, and I was getting more frantic every second and wondering if buttering my finger would help or if Dad had a hacksaw anywhere in the house and if I could cut through the stupid ring without sawing my finger off or if I was going to be stuck with this thing on my finger for the rest of my life and if it was *really* dangerous or—

Then, as suddenly as the ring had gone through its little quick change routine, *I* went through one, too. At least something inside of my head did, and all of a sudden I wasn't trying to pull the ring off anymore.

Again it was sort of like an optical illusion, only this time it all happened inside my head, in my thoughts. One second I was practically panicked out of my mind, thinking how incredibly dumb it had been to put the thing on my finger in the first place, but the next second, the panic was all gone. Everything was okay.

I was still thinking how dumb it had been to put the thing on in the first place, but mostly I was thinking something like, *It's only a ring, so what can it hurt?*

At least there was a little voice in my head saying something like that. I'm not sure it was really *me*, though.

Anyway, I left the ring on—as if I had a choice!—and finished soaking up what water I could from the rug. Then I went to my room and started looking through the half dozen tests Ms. Armour had already given us in English this semester. Hulk, who had finished his washing routine, followed me in and of course hopped up on the little desk Dad had given me a couple of years before and planted all twenty of his hairy pounds on the stack of test papers.

I'd set Hulk on the floor maybe half a dozen times and had managed to review all of half a page of the first test when my finger started tingling, like it was going to sleep.

Yes, the finger with the ring. What else?

For a couple of seconds, panic hit me again, just like it had when I'd first put the ring on. I could just imagine some kind of chemical inside the ring eating away at my finger, or maybe my finger turning blurry like the ring had been at first, or maybe even disappearing or falling off.

But then the panic was gone, just like before. And the tingling was gone, too.

At least it was gone from my finger. The rest of me started feeling weird, though. It wasn't a tingle, just a sort of twitchy feeling, kind of like the feeling you get when it's the last class period of the day and you're in study hall and you have all your lessons done and the weather is just perfect out there on the other side of the window, and there's nothing you'd like better than to hop on your bike and ride off somewhere.

That's the sort of twitchy feeling it was, only there was a difference.

And the difference was, I didn't feel like riding off just anywhere. I felt like riding off to the southwest.

The trouble is, there's nothing much you can reach on a bicycle—or on foot, for that matter—in that direction. There's another few blocks of houses, and then there's a few acres of almost-swamp and then there's Gradwohl's Creek. Beyond that, on the dry side of the creek, there's a campground the Boy Scouts and a bunch of other groups use every so often, but the nearest bridge is a half mile upstream. So, unless I wanted to go wading, there was just no way I could go very far southwest, on my bike or off it.

But that's what I felt like doing, no matter how dumb or illogical it sounds.

What's more, I was actually down on the porch, un-chaining the ten-speed, when Mom came home five minutes later, dragging Walter, my seven-year-old brother. And if you're wondering why I haven't mentioned *him* before, well, I try not to think about Walter any more than I have to. It's not that he's a pain in the neck or anything like that, although he is now and then. I mean, as brothers e's okay, not like Dave Shaeffer's little brother Jerry. only four, and there's nothing that gives him a bigger bang than to sneak up behind Dave and let go with what he thinks is a blood-curdling scream but which is really sort of a loud, squeaky giggle, since the second he starts to scream, he starts thinking how funny it's going to be and he starts giggling instead of screaming.

Anyway, Walter's nothing like that. For one thing, like I said, he's seven, and even when he was four, he didn't do dumb things like that. And ever since we moved to this new house a couple of years ago, he's had his own room, so he doesn't get in the way *too* much, except that Mom keeps telling me I'm going to be old enough to start "babysitting" with him before long, which is a pretty grim thought.

Anyway, Mom and Walter came home, which side-tracked this dumb impulse I had to ride off into the swamp. Mom, I saw right off, was practically glowing, and as she came up onto the porch, she gave me a big hug, almost lifting me off my feet. Walter just stood on the steps and watched with one of his "Now-it's-your-turn-to-put-up-with-it" looks.

"I sold the old Diefenbacher place," she said when she put me down. "Can you believe it? The Diefenbacher place!"

Now I don't normally pay much attention to what they sell at Carbuncle, but even I know about the Diefenbacher place, mainly because it's been deserted for as long as I can remember, and Kathy and I and half the kids in the county have been out there "exploring" at one time or another. It's a couple miles southwest of town, not far from where Gradwohl's Creek goes into the lake. It's way back at the end of a little lane that's all grown

25

over, and the land itself is turning into swamp or something. Bad drainage, Mom said once. Anyway, it's not worth much, and nobody had so much as made an offer on it before.

"Who bought it?" I asked. Whoever it was, they'd probably put up some NO TRESPASSING signs first thing.

"Someone named Johnson," Mom said, still grinning. "He's not from around here, but he *says* he's got the money to pay cash, and that's what counts. He just walked into the office this afternoon, and I was the only one there, so—"

She stopped. "Come on," she said, glancing toward the living room where Hulk sat watching us with his "Isn't-it-suppertime-*yet?*" look. "Cal, you give the beast in there something to tide him over till supper, and we'll pick your father up at work and go celebrate. How does that sound?"

It sounded great, and I said so. "Can we go to Bjornsen's?" I asked.

Mom made a face, but she said okay. Bjornsen's is over in Cranston, run by someone named Arne Bjornsen, and it's my favorite place to eat. Its whole name is Bjornsen's Swedish Pizza Emporium, and it's the only place I know of where you can get a pizza with some sort of secret ingredient that gives it a chocolatey flavor mixed in with the pepperoni and all the rest. It's sort of hard to imagine, but it's great. Really.

Anyway, we were on our way in three or four minutes, heading out to Harding to pick up Dad. I'd almost completely forgotten about the ring and the tingling.

But then, after we'd called Dad on the plant phone and

were waiting at the guard's desk in the lobby for Dad to lock his stuff up and come out to meet us, I got reminded. My finger all of a sudden felt like someone had stuck a couple hundred teeny-tiny needles into it. It didn't hurt, it was just prickly, and it was gone almost as soon as it came.

But as soon as it ended, I got a feeling that made the twitchy ones I'd had before feel like nothing. I was turned around and half way to the door to the parking lot before I caught myself and stopped, which wasn't all that easy.

But I managed, just barely. Mom didn't seem to notice I was jumpier than usual, or if she did, maybe she just thought I was anxious to get to Bjornsen's. Walter was another matter, though. He hardly took his eyes off me, but at least he didn't say anything.

Then Dad showed up, and we were on our way. And my twitchiness eased off a little, mainly because, I suppose, we were moving, and moving in the right direction at that. At least that's what I figured out later. Right then, I didn't have *any* idea what was going on.

Dad's name, by the way, is Harrison. Harrison Willeford, and if anyone calls him "Harry," he gives them a funny look. Like me, he's got a crew cut, although Mom keeps telling him his hair's getting too thin on top for it, but he hasn't paid any attention yet.

Anyway, he gave Mom a big hug when she told him about the Diefenbacher deal, and he made a face and looked sideways at me when she said we were going to Bjornsen's. He at least tasted my pizza there once, which is more than Mom or anyone else has ever done. After he tasted it, he just shook his head and drank a whole glass of water and never tried it again, but he *did* taste it.

We were out on the highway then, and Mom was giving Dad more details about the sale, and he was sounding more and more curious about the guy who bought it. In the end, since it was only a couple of miles out of the way and it was still pretty early for supper, they decided to swing by the Diefenbacher place and see if Johnson or someone was around.

Now normally any kind of delay like this would've gotten me all antsy, especially when Bjornsen's was what was getting delayed, but this time it didn't. In fact, the closer we got to the Diefenbacher place, the more it seemed like a good idea. Mainly because it kept looking more and more like that was right where all my twitchy feelings would've taken me anyway.

3

"Mom, He Looks Funny!"

The long lane leading from the road back to the Diefenbacher place looked pretty much the way I remembered it from last summer, the last time Kathy and I had been out there. The weeds were so high, if it hadn't been for the rusty, sagging fence along each side, you wouldn't even know there was a lane there.

"How did you and your Mr. Johnson get back here to look the place over?" Dad asked as Mom maneuvered us slowly down the lane. "It doesn't look like anyone's been through here for ages."

"He said he'd already seen it. We just drove past on the road back there, just to be sure this was really the place he had in mind." She shrugged. "It was."

"And he didn't say *why* he wanted it?"

Mom shook her head. "You know what they say about gift horses. Or houses, in this case."

Dad didn't say anything for another minute, while Mom got the car through a batch of thistles that came right up over the hood, but then he sighed. "Some government foolishness, I'll bet. Wouldn't be surprised if it was the CIA."

"What would the government want with *this* place?" Mom asked.

"What would *anyone* want with it? Anyone in his right mind, that is."

By then we'd reached what I guess you'd call the "front yard." It looked pretty much like the lane, except it was wider and had a bunch of trees mixed in with the weeds. One big oak looked like it was a hundred feet tall, and a weeping willow at the side of the house looked like something out of a Louisiana bayou. I'd seen it all when Kathy and I'd been out here last summer, but it looked weirder now. Or it seemed to, anyway, what with that twitchy feeling still bugging me.

Then, for just a second, I thought I saw something move behind one of the broken windows. And for another second, I felt like getting out of the car. I even had my hand on the door, but I pulled it back. Nobody else had any kind of feeling like that, though, I guess. At least no one else made any move to get out.

And I just sat there in the back seat, feeling twitchy. And Walter, I noticed, wasn't taking his eyes off me for a second, not even while Mom struggled to get the car turned around and almost scraped the oak tree.

"Definitely the government," Dad said as the car lurched out of the weeds and back onto the road at the end of the lane. "Very definitely the government."

Even with our little detour, we got to Bjornsen's before it started filling up for supper. Mr. Bjornsen himself, a few years older and a lot of pounds heavier than Dad, came out and took our orders. He winked at me when he asked if I wanted the "usual special." Walter, of course, insisted on a hamburger.

Meanwhile, my twitchy feelings had just about gone away, and without them to sidetrack me, I started getting nervous all over again. I mean, *nothing* that had happened to me since I tossed that water on Hulk and Generic had made any sense at *all*. And the fact that I'd stayed relatively calm through the whole thing made the least sense of anything. Oh, I'd had a couple panicky moments, but that's all they had been—moments. The rest of the time—well, sure, I knew that weird things were happening to me. I could hardly miss them without being blind. But they hadn't really upset me except, like I said, those two or three times.

And besides the major weirdnesses, like the disappearing cat and the ring that changed size and my own twitchiness, there were some minor ones. Like the fact that Walter hadn't taken his eyes off me. Like the fact that nobody had said anything about the ring, which was so big and clunky I don't see how they could miss it.

Anyway, the whole thing was almost enough to keep me from enjoying the pizza. Almost, but not quite.

But then, when we'd finished eating and Mom was paying the cashier, my finger got all prickly for a couple seconds and the twitchiness hit me again. Just like that, in four or five seconds at the most, and it was almost as bad as when we'd been waiting for Dad in the Harding lobby. I managed to hold back, but just barely.

And then, when we all went out into the parking lot, it only got worse, and I started wondering if maybe I was really going batty. I mean, none of this tingling or twitchiness or *anything* was even the least bit logical. I was just starting to work up the nerve to say something to Mom or Dad about it when she started waving at someone.

"Mr. Johnson!" she said, almost yelling. "What a surprise."

And there, between a couple of cars in the next row, was this guy in a black suit. And a hat. Mom started leading us all toward him, still talking.

The thing was, Mr. Johnson wasn't looking at Mom. He was looking at *me*. At the ring. I swear.

But then, all of a sudden, Walter came to a dead stop. His eyes may not have bugged out, but they were as big as I'd ever seen them. He grabbed Mom's hand, something I hadn't seen him do voluntarily for at least a year and a half.

"Mom," he said in that voice of his that sounds like a steam whistle and carries for about a quarter of a mile, "he looks funny!"

That got Johnson's attention off me and the ring, fast. His expression—actually, he didn't have all that much of an expression to begin with—didn't change, but *something* did.

"Excuse me, but I must go," Johnson said, and he did. Go, I mean.

"Walter!" Mom said. "You apologize this minute!"

And then, calling after Mr. Johnson, "I'm sorry, Mr. Johnson, but you know how children are."

"But he *did* look funny," Walter insisted. "And I'm scared!"

But he didn't apologize, mainly because we couldn't find Mr. Johnson to apologize to. Not that Mom didn't try, but Johnson was just gone. He didn't go into Bjornsen's, and he didn't drive away in a car unless he was hiding in someone's trunk. He just wasn't there anymore.

"I hope," Mom said with a glare at Walter as we finally climbed back into our own car, "you didn't insult the poor man so much I'll lose my commission!"

4

"I Suppose It's One of Those Magic Watchamacallits."

O n the way back home, we stopped at the Harding parking lot so Dad could pick up his car, and I rode the rest of the way home with him. A half dozen times, I had my mouth open to tell him about the ring and the tingles and the vanishing cat, but it was all so totally illogical, I just couldn't get the words to come out. Instead, he asked me if I was ready for my exams next week, and I told him I figured I was, pretty much, and that's the way it went.

I got through the evening without any more tingles or twitches, and several times I almost took the ring off, but I never quite managed *that*, either.

I did manage to sleep a little, though, and Saturday morning I decided that the only logical thing to do was to talk to Kathy about it. If there was one person who could make sense out of things that just plain didn't make sense, it was her. And even if she couldn't, she'd always have some sort of idea for something to do.

When I got to her block, she was coming up the sidewalk with Mastodon on a leash. Mastodon is the Entsmingers' dog, or at least that's what Kathy says. He's a dog like Hulk's a cat, only more so. He's the biggest, hairiest thing I've ever seen outside a zoo, kind of like his namesake, only without the trunk and tusks. Usually he jumps up and puts his paws on my shoulders and slobbers on me, but this time he kept all four feet on the ground. Kathy, as usual, was wearing faded jeans and sneakers, this time with a Darth Vader sweatshirt.

While we walked back to her house and put Mastodon in the fenced-in back yard, I told her about the cat fight and the ring. I didn't mention what the cat had turned into.

"What ring?" she asked. "What's it look like?"

"Like this," I said, holding my finger out for her.

"Like what?" she asked, glancing at my outstretched hand and then frowning at me.

"Like *this*," I repeated, and put the ring practically under her nose. "This is it, right here on my finger. See?"

She glanced at my finger again, really frowning this time, and then she looked up at me. "Calvin, what are you talking about?"

"This ring, right there!" I said, holding the ring about six inches in front of her nose and tapping it with a finger of my other hand.

Still frowning, she looked where I was pointing. For two or three seconds, she just looked, and the frown got deeper, but then, all of a sudden, her eyes got really wide and her mouth popped open.

"Wow!" she said. "That was really great, Calvin! How'd you do it?"

"Do it? Do what?"

"Come on, Calvin! How'd you do it?"

"Kathy, I don't know what you're talking about. *What did I do?*" I was starting to feel panicky again.

Kathy just stared at me. "That ring," she said finally, sounding sort of ticked off. "How'd you do it?"

"Do *what?*"

"Make it appear on your finger like you just did!"

"Appear?"

She stared at me for a couple more seconds, and she was starting to look downright exasperated. "What are you trying to pull, Calvin Willeford? You show me that really neat trick, and now you're acting like you don't know what I'm talking about. Look, if you don't want to tell me, you don't have to!" She started to turn away, but only part way.

I looked at the ring myself, and I got a little sinking feeling in my stomach. *I* hadn't been able to see it at first, there on the rug, at least not until I'd felt it under the paper towel and then actually picked it up. And Mom and Dad hadn't said a word about it all yesterday evening or even this morning at breakfast. Like *they* hadn't been able to see it either.

"The ring just—just appeared?" I asked. "Out of thin air?"

"As if you didn't know!" Kathy turned to look at me again. If eyes really did that sort of thing, hers would've been flashing. As it is, they looked a lot brighter green than they usually did, although that's probably just because she was leaning so close to me. Her freckles sort of stood out more than usual, too.

"One second it wasn't there?" I asked. "And the next second it was?"

Her whole head bobbed up and down as she nodded. "Now how did you do it? I suppose it's one of those magic watchamacallits you saw advertised on the back of a comic book or something."

I shook my head. "I told you, I found it."

"All right, but how did you make it appear all of a sudden like that?"

"I didn't."

"What's *that* supposed to mean?"

"I didn't make the ring appear, or anything else. I—"

"That's *your* finger, isn't it?" she asked, pointing.

"Yes, but— Look, Kathy, I didn't *do* anything with that ring!"

We were in her front yard, and right about then Kathy's mother came out. She had her keys in her hand and was heading toward the little VW parked at the curb.

"Come on," I said, "let's show it to your mother and see if *she* can see it."

"Of course she can see it, now that you've made it appear!"

"Just keep your eye on the ring, just to make sure it doesn't disappear, then," I said, and ran over to Kathy's mother.

37

"Good morning, Mrs. Entsminger," I said.

"Why Calvin, good morning. What brings you around so early?"

"I had something to show Kathy, something I found yesterday. And she thought you might like to see it, too."

She smiled like she wasn't sure what was coming next. "That's nice, Calvin, but I have to be at—"

"This ring," I said, holding my hand out in front of her like I had with Kathy a minute before. "We were just wondering if you'd ever seen one like it before."

She looked at my hand, and now she looked like she not only wasn't sure what was coming next but was pretty sure she wasn't going to like it, whatever it was. "Yes, Calvin? Where is this ring you wanted to show me?"

I could almost hear Kathy blink, and then she reached out and touched the ring with her finger. "Right here, Mom. The ring's right here on his finger."

Mrs. Entsminger stared at my finger, just the way Kathy had before. Then her eyes got wider, and she sort of twitched backward maybe half an inch.

"Oh," she said, "*that* ring. I—I almost didn't see it at first."

Which was sort of what I was expecting, but it still shook me up a little. People just couldn't see the ring until I practically hit them over the head with it. At least that's the way it seemed to work with Kathy and her mother, and it must've been the same way with Mom and Dad last night. Only they never *did* see it, since I didn't even tell them about it, let alone shove it under their noses.

Kathy's fingers dug into my arm as her mother made her excuses and hurried to her car.

"You did it again, didn't you?" Kathy said, giving me an accusing look.

I shook my head. "Whatever happened, *I* didn't do it."

So we went around to the back yard where her father was getting the lawn mower out of the garage and was glad for any interruption. I did the same thing I'd done with Mrs. Entsminger, only this time I had Kathy hang onto the ring—and my finger—the whole time.

But it didn't make any difference. It wasn't until her father stared at my finger from eight or ten inches away that he "noticed" the ring.

"Not a bad trick, kids," he said, grinning. "I don't suppose you could make some of this grass disappear the same way?"

Back at the front of the house, Kathy was still giving me dirty looks, but she was starting to look a little nervous, too. But then, just when she looked like she was winding up for another "How did you do it?" my finger got all prickly again. When I told her about it and about the "twitchiness" that always followed, she brightened.

"Sort of like a hunch, you mean?" she asked. "You get a 'hunch' you oughta go north or south or right or left? That sort of thing?"

"Something like that," I admitted. "But—"

"And you ended up at the old Diefenbacher place? And the parking lot at Bjornsen's?"

"Yeah, but—"

"So where's it telling you to go this time?"

39

I pointed in the general direction of downtown.

"Well," she said, "that's better than the Diefenbacher place. Let's go."

"Go? Where?"

"Wherever that thing is telling you to go. Where else?"

"But—"

"Come on, Calvin. How do you expect to find out what's going on if you just stand around here and don't follow your hunches?"

"They're not hunches, they're just twitches."

"Whatever they are, they want you to go in this direction, so let's go. Before they get tired of waiting and send someone to get you," she added with the same deadpan look she'd given me when she'd compared my life to a squashed bottle cap.

So we went. Since my bike was back at home, two blocks in the other direction, we walked. Kathy watched me every step of the way, sort of like Walter had watched me yesterday, only with a determined look. And she kept watching the ring, too, like she was expecting it to disappear or start glowing or talking or something. None of which, by the way, would've really surprised me, not after the way things had been going.

We were a couple of blocks from Main Street when I saw Mr. Johnson. Or I should say, I saw someone I *thought* was Mr. Johnson. After all, who else in East Gradwohl would be wearing not only a black suit but that same, dark, wide-brimmed hat?

A few seconds later, however, I saw a *second* Mr. Johnson, about three feet away from the first. A second black suit and dark hat, and I wondered why I hadn't seen the second one right away.

Unless I was seeing double, I thought, and shook my head. But neither one disappeared. They were about a hundred feet away, standing on the sidewalk just past the new jail, which looks more like a library than a jail, what with the way it's spread out over half a block with a big lawn with shrubs and everything. Like Mr. Johnson, or whoever it was I'd seen in Bjornsen's parking lot, their faces were hard to see, sort of like they were in shadows, even when they faced the sun, which they were doing now.

When I pointed them out, Kathy stared at them a second. "Where'd *they* come from?" she asked with a frown. "They weren't there a second ago. Are they what that compass of yours is pointing you at?"

I nodded. I hadn't said anything about it yet, but the twitchy feeling had been getting stronger all the time, and now it was almost as strong as it had been over at Bjornsen's. It was all I could do to keep from running across the street to where the two black suits were standing.

"So what are we waiting for?" Kathy asked, grabbing my hand and heading directly toward them.

"Now wait a minute!" I began, but Kathy wasn't paying attention to anything but the suits. I held back enough to keep her from galloping, but that was all.

We got to the other side of the street, maybe thirty feet from the suits, right in front of the walkway that led up to the front door of the jail, when one of the suits turned in our direction. I still couldn't see his face very well, but I could tell he was looking at the ring.

Kathy waved. "Hey, Mr. Johnson," she called.

With that, it was just like Friday afternoon at Bjornsen's, except there were two suits instead of one. The suit that had been looking in our direction made a quick turn and headed in the opposite direction, and the other suit followed without a word.

Kathy tried to start running, but I was still hanging back. Then she let go of my hand and she *did* start running, but by then the two suits had reached the alley, which was cut off from the jail lawn by six-foot-high hedges.

When I reached the alley, Kathy was standing about ten feet in, looking around.

"Where'd they go?" I asked.

"What's that compass of yours say?" she asked.

And that's when I realized it wasn't saying *anything*. The twitchiness, the hunch, whatever you want to call it, was gone.

And it had disappeared, now that I thought about it, about a second and a half *after* the two black suits had ducked around the hedge and into the alley and out of sight.

· 5 ·

"Vampires Wear Tuxedos, Not Suits."

We were poking around in the bushes that line the alley next to the jail when I heard footsteps behind us. I don't know about Kathy, but I pretty much froze, figuring it was Sheriff Pippenger coming out to see what we were up to. And put a stop to it. He's really a sourpuss, at least whenever any kids are around. I've never seen him so much as crack a smile, and neither has anyone else at school. And I'd never dare smile while he was around, that's for sure. He'd probably think I was up to something.

"Looking for something, kids?" a voice asked, and I came unfroze when I realized it wasn't Pippenger after all.

It was Phil Hostetler, the chief deputy. He's just the

opposite of the sheriff, real easygoing, almost always smiling. He also weighs probably three hundred pounds, which is about two hundred more than Pippenger, even if they are both about the same height, around six feet like Dad. But it isn't fat, or at least not much of it is. Hostetler used to be a wrestler in college, and an awful lot of what looks like flab is really muscle. I mean, he can pick kids heavier than me up with one hand and hold them out at arm's length without looking like he's even working at it, which he likes to demonstrate every so often. And which a lot of the kids like to *see* him demonstrate. They even make a sort of game out of it, putting weights in their pockets just to see if they can make him work up a sweat. So far, nobody has.

Incidentally, this weight-lifting business is something else that turned out to be pretty important later on, like that fake boulder of Kathy's. Not to mention the fact that Hostetler used to be sheriff, back before Pippenger beat him in the last election, and he's planning to run again this fall. Needless to say, everyone at school—except for maybe a couple of the grouchier teachers—are on Hostetler's side. Anyway, all this stuff does come together after awhile, believe it or not. With a lot of help from Kathy, of course.

But like I said before I got sidetracked, it was Hostetler behind us, not Pippenger, and all he really did was ask us what we were looking for and then nod while we made lame excuses. You could tell he didn't believe a word we said, but he just nodded with that little half grin of his and said, "That's real interesting. But you better not let

Pip catch you out here unless you put together a lot better story than this one."

With a wave, he wandered back toward the jail, leaving us both feeling sort of lucky. And dumb.

As we walked away ourselves, Kathy looked at the ring again. "That thing hasn't given you any more 'hunches,' has it?"

"Not a thing since those two suits disappeared. Why?"

"Are you really *trying?*"

"Trying what?"

"You know! Trying to get a 'hunch,' or a twitch, or whatever you call them."

I shook my head. "I don't think 'trying' has anything to do with it."

"Here," she said, holding her hand out, "let *me* try it."

I started to say "sure," but then I remembered how last night I'd thought about taking the ring off a half dozen times but hadn't been able to quite make it. It was like something—something in my head—always kept me from doing it, just like it'd been something in my head that had probably gotten me to put the thing on in the first place.

Okay, I thought, *if I can't take it off myself, maybe somebody else can. Somebody like Kathy.*

"Here," I said, holding my hand out stiffly, "take it if you want it."

She looked at me kind of funny, but she didn't waste any time. She grabbed my hand in one of hers and started pulling at the ring with the other. The ring didn't come off easily, and all the time she was pulling and tugging, I

45

had to keep a pretty tight hold on myself to keep from jerking my hand away from her. My finger didn't tingle or anything like that, but I did feel more than a little weird. I mean, I didn't really *want* to pull my hand back so she couldn't get the ring off my finger, but I kept feeling like I *should* want to, if that makes any sense at all.

Anyway, no matter what I felt like, she finally got the ring off. I looked at it, laying there in her hand.

"It's all fuzzy again," I said.

And it was. It was just like it had been when I'd first picked it up—big and clunky and blurry. Out of focus.

She looked at it and sort of twitched, or maybe shivered. For a few seconds, I thought she wasn't going to do anything at all, that she was just going to let it lie there or maybe give it back to me, but I should've known better. If there's one thing Kathy never has, it's second thoughts. Or if she does, she never lets them get in the way of anything she wants to do.

She put the ring on.

Her fingers aren't much smaller than mine, so the ring hung on her finger about the way it had on mine at first. There was practically room for a second finger inside it.

"How long does it take to shrink down so it fits me?" she asked when nothing had happened for ten or fifteen seconds.

"Not this long," I said.

We kept on watching, at least another minute, but still nothing happened. She twitched her finger, and the ring, blur and all, whirled around like a tiny hula hoop.

"Maybe there's a secret button or something," she

said, poking at the inside of the ring, then the outside. But still nothing happened.

"Maybe it needs a new battery," I said, thinking of the watch that had conked out on me last week.

She poked some more. She even gave it a good, solid wack on a parking meter, but nothing happened except that the meter gave a click and lost ten minutes, which probably wouldn't make the guy who parked there any too happy.

"Here," she said, handing it back to me. "You try it again."

I looked at it, and the blurriness almost hurt my eyes. Logic—or caution, which is a form of logic, as far as I'm concerned—told me I shouldn't put it back on, now that it was finally off. Logically, what I should do was take it home and show it to Dad, who could maybe get it analyzed by someone at Harding. Except, if the ring turned out to be something *really* interesting or weird, whoever Dad showed it to at Harding would turn it over to the government, and they would classify it top secret or something, and that would be the last I'd ever see of it. Or even *hear* of it. They probably wouldn't *ever* tell me what it really was, even if they *did* find out.

So I put it back on my finger.

And while Kathy and I watched as closely as we could, the ring went through the same optical illusion routine it had gone through before. The next thing we knew, it was as solid-looking as ever, and it fit my finger perfectly.

"Guess it must be tuned just to you," Kathy said, and I got a little shiver at the thought.

But then my finger started tingling again.

I must've jumped or made a noise or something, because the next thing I knew, Kathy was looking at me with a frown. "It's doing it again, isn't it?" she asked.

I just nodded and waited for the twitchiness to take over from the tingle. In maybe ten or fifteen seconds, it did.

"Where to now?" Kathy wanted to know.

But it was sort of weak this time, like the battery was wearing down.

"Back this way," I said finally, pointing north along Maple Street.

A half hour later, we came to the Third Street Church, almost at the edge of town.

"In there?" Kathy asked, pointing at the big double doors at the top of the steps.

"I think so," I said. The feeling was pretty strong now, a lot stronger than it had been at first.

Before we could do anything, though, the doors opened and dozens of people started coming out, all dressed in suits and ties and that sort of thing. And then Kathy was pointing to a car parked across the street. There was a JUST MARRIED sign wired on the back of the trunk, and about the time I saw that, the bride and groom, whoever they were, came out of the church.

And on the edge of the crowd watching the whole thing was another black suit. Even with practically every man in the crowd wearing a suit, this guy stood out. For one thing, he was the only one wearing a hat, and I wondered if he'd been wearing it inside the church.

Anyway, Kathy saw him, too, and we started toward him. We were ten or fifteen feet away when he saw us.

First, when he saw the ring, he started moving toward me, but then he saw Kathy, who was staring right at him.

He turned and ducked into the crowd. Or "melted" into it.

Anyway, whether he ducked or melted or just plain flew away, he was gone, and a few seconds later, so was my "feeling."

This time, Kathy asked the first three or four people she ran into if they remembered seeing the man, but hardly anyone did. One woman vaguely remembered someone sitting in the back of the church during the ceremony, "with his hat on, for goodness sake!" But she hadn't seen him outside.

As we started back toward the center of town, Kathy looked thoughtful for a couple of blocks, and then, suddenly, her eyes widened, about like they had when the ring "appeared" for her on my finger.

She grinned until her eyes crinkled up. "UFOs!" she said, and a couple people across the street frowned in our direction.

"UFOs?"

"Sure!" she said. "That's where these guys in the suits are coming from—UFOs!"

"You mean flying saucers? From outer space?"

"What other kind do you know about?"

"That's crazy! What ever gave you an idea like that?"

"I read about them somewhere. And they—"

"*Read* about them? Where?"

"I don't remember, exactly. It was in some magazine Dad had. We were cleaning out the garage and I was carting these stacks of magazines out to the sidewalk for some paper drive truck to pick up, only there was something on the cover of this one magazine about how your next door neighbor could be from outer space, so I pulled it out and read it and—" She stopped for breath.

"And it says guys from UFOs wear black suits?" I asked. "Aren't you getting aliens mixed up with vampires?"

"Vampires wear tuxedos, not suits. Don't you know anything?"

"You know what I mean. Who ever heard of anyone from outer space wearing a black suit?"

"I suppose *you* think they're all little green men or monsters or something like that."

"I didn't say that. But *black suits*—"

"I don't suppose you've ever even *heard* of Grey Barker."

"What's that supposed to be, some kind of dog?"

"Very funny. As a matter of fact, it's the man who wrote the article. Or maybe the guy the article was about, I'm not sure. But I remembered the name because it sounded so funny. Anyway, he used to write about UFOs back in prehistoric times, back in the forties or fifties. And he met a lot of people from UFOs, and they—"

"Kathy! Come on!"

"Okay, he *said* he met a lot of people from UFOs. The thing is, he said they all looked alike, and they all wore black suits!"

"Why?"

"How should I know? Maybe they all shopped at the same store. Anyway, it didn't say. It just said they *did*."

"You sure it wasn't men in *white* suits? With nets?"

"All I know is what it said in the article. And what it said was that people that came here in UFOs were all dressed in black suits when they came around to visit Barker or his friends or whoever it was they were visiting. And now they're visiting you and they're still wearing their black suits."

"This is all crazy," I said. "Look, I don't even *believe* in UFOs! They're not logical!"

"So I suppose that ring of yours *is* logical, Mr. Spock?"

"I didn't say that, but— Look, even if UFOs did exist, and even if they did send out people in black suits, why would they send them here? And what do they have to do with this ring?"

"They probably made it." Her grin widened. "Who else could make something that acts like that thing does? All blurry one second and solid as anything the next. And the way it leads you to the suits—"

"Who said it leads me to *anything*?"

"*Something* is leading you to them."

"But—"

"I bet it's a detector, an alien detector! Whenever you get close to one, it leads you right to him!"

"That's *really* crazy!"

"Sure it is, but I bet that's what it is, anyway!"

"But look, even if UFOs did exist, what was an—an 'alien detector' doing on our rug?"

"It was left by someone who wants you to detect aliens, what else?"

"If someone wants me to detect aliens, why didn't he just give the ring to me and tell me how to use it and what it's for. It would be pretty dumb to just leave it lying on the floor that way."

"Would you have believed anyone who handed you a ring and said it was an alien detector?"

"Of course not!"

"So they just left it there and let you find it and find out for yourself what it does. Or maybe," she added with another crinkly grin, "*maybe* that cat left it! Maybe they can control animals' minds, and they gave this cat the ring and made it follow you home but that monster of yours jumped on it and you tried to drown it and it didn't have time to—"

All of a sudden she wasn't talking anymore, she was just looking at me. And looking suspicious.

"Calvin!" she said. "You've got that look on your face again."

"What look?"

"You know what I mean! It's that look you get when you're trying not to tell me something. Now what is it?"

I was quiet a few seconds, but then I sighed. She was right. My face is like Pinocchio's nose. Whenever I try to say anything that isn't within a couple millimeters of the total truth, my face practically breaks out in flashing lights. If I was a spy, I'd last maybe eighteen or nineteen seconds.

"Okay," I said, and then I told her about the cat and its disappearance and its reappearance and its escape. Her eyes got wider with each sentence.

"Wow!" she said when I finished. "I'll bet that was one of the *other* aliens!"

"Other aliens? *What* other aliens?"

"Don't you see? There must be *two* groups of them! The ones that wear black suits and the ones disguised as cats! And when you threw water on him, his disguise broke down!"

"But what was he doing in our house in the first place?"

"How should I know? Maybe he was looking for your Dad. He makes those computer watchamacallits they use in spaceships, doesn't he?"

"They're space *probes*, not space *ships*, and besides, what does that have to do with anything?"

She shrugged. "Maybe they've got a message for him. Or maybe they were going to recruit him for their side, and they wanted to give him this ring so he could tell them when anyone from the other side was around, and—"

"Come on, Kathy! That's crazy. Why would someone who can build UFOs and all that stuff want to 'recruit' a human? What could one of us possibly do that they couldn't already do better?"

"Just because they can build spaceships doesn't mean they can do *everything*. They probably need a *lot* of help."

Which, I have to admit, stopped me. Because she was probably right. Dad had said the same sort of thing, about how we really aren't any brighter than people were three thousand years ago. Sure, we've got all kinds of gadgets like jet planes and computers and television, but that's not because we're any smarter. We're just lucky we're living now instead of then, and we've got all these gadgets.

So just because someone was from outer space, he didn't have to be any brighter than we were, any more than he had to be a slime monster or a Klingon.

But if they *were* from outer space and they wanted help, why were they always running away from me?

So I asked Kathy.

"The ones in the suits aren't the ones that need help," she said. "It's the ones who disguise themselves as cats. The ones in the suits probably don't want anyone to know who they are, so they run away whenever they see anyone who knows who they are. Or anyone who has an alien detector. Or maybe it's more than just a detector. Maybe it's got something in it that scares them off."

"Sure, an alien repellent, like a bug spray."

"Well, why not? It's probably some kind of protective field. Or maybe," she said suddenly, "it's not *you* they're running away from!"

"Who else?"

"Well, I was watching that last one, and he didn't start running until he saw *me* looking at him. And from what you said about the one yesterday, he didn't run away until your twerpy little brother insulted him."

Which was, now that I thought of it, right enough. "You mean more than one person looking at them scares them off?"

She shrugged again. "There's one way to find out. Next time you see one, I'll stay out of the way. *You* go up to him and see what you can find out."

I blinked. She must really be serious about this, I thought. If there was anything Kathy never did voluntarily, it was stay out of the way.

Before I had much time to think about it, though, my finger got all prickly again, and I found myself being pointed back toward downtown.

"It's happening again, isn't it?" Kathy asked suspiciously as she saw me look around.

I nodded.

"So get going. Just don't go so fast you lose me."

So I went.

"You *Pay* Someone to *Lie* to You?"

Twenty minutes later I was jogging along Main Street past the Rialto Theater's rusty marquee. The twitchiness was getting stronger all the time, and each time I looked over my shoulder, I could see Kathy fifty feet behind me.

UFOs? Black suits from outer space, for crying out loud?

But the "cat" *had* disappeared, and something else *had* appeared in its place. Something *very* else. And I *was* getting these tingles and twitches and was finding all these black suits. Considering all that, Kathy's explanation made as much sense as anything I could think of, which was nothing at all, except to wonder if I really *was* going crazy.

But then, about the time I'd gone over the same stuff seven or eight times, I saw another black suit. This one was standing on the sidewalk in front of Grimsby's Department Store watching the TV set Grimsby always has hooked up in the window.

I held my hand up to signal Kathy. For a minute or so, I just stood there across the street watching the suit watch the TV set. I couldn't tell for sure what was on, but it looked like a movie, even if it was Saturday morning. Grimsby probably had the set hooked up to a video recorder. He sold them and had movies you could rent and play on them.

Looking back, I saw Kathy standing about forty feet away. She was making faces and urging me to get moving.

Carefully, I crossed the street and stopped at the edge of the sidewalk, maybe eight or ten feet behind the suit. I stood there for another minute at least, working up the nerve to cross those last few feet. My twitchiness or hunch or whatever was practically buried under just plain old nervousness, now that Kathy'd gotten me to thinking about UFOs and aliens.

But finally I took another couple of steps and then a couple more, and at last I was standing next to the suit, close enough to reach out and touch it, and it hadn't disappeared. The face wasn't blurry, but it *was* in a shadow. And it did look like what little I'd seen of Mr. Johnson's face the day before—very plain, without any wrinkles at all. And no expression.

Like, I suddenly thought with another sinking feeling, the cat. The generic cat. This guy, whoever or whatever he was, looked sort of like a generic man, and I wondered what would appear in his place if he disappeared like the cat.

If I'd been alone, if Kathy hadn't been across the street practically hopping up and down with impatience, I would've turned around and walked away. But I wasn't, she was, and I didn't.

"Excuse me," I said, "but are you Mr. Johnson?"

For a second or two, it was like he didn't hear me, but then he turned to look down at me. His tie, I could see now, was gray. And for half a second or something like that, he looked down at the ring.

"What are these people doing?" he asked, pointing at the TV set in the window. His voice was sort of neutral, too, like the rest of him. And the way his lips moved looked funny.

"If you *aren't* Mr. Johnson, who are you?"

He twitched slightly, and then he frowned, sort of. "What are these people doing?" he repeated, pointing at the TV set again. His voice sounded different, maybe a little deeper. And I realized why the way his lips moved looked funny. The movements didn't quite match the words he was saying. It was like those foreign movies where they dub in English dialogue, only this wasn't quite that bad.

"What are these people doing?" he asked for a third time, and this time I felt my finger tingle again.

And all of a sudden I felt like answering him. The same way I'd felt like walking in a certain direction before, now I felt like answering him.

I looked at the TV set. Like I'd thought before, it was

showing a movie, one I'd seen last winter on TV. It was one of those crime movies where the crooks spend half the movie planning how to rob a bank or something and then spend the second half trying to actually rob it but getting everything goofed up.

"They're getting ready to rob a bank," I said.

"That is what I thought. But why are they letting someone take their pictures and broadcast them?"

I blinked. "What?"

"I said, why are they letting someone take their pictures and broadcast them? It would seem that such plans should be kept secret."

"They *are* being kept secret." I pointed at the TV set, where three of the crooks were sitting around a table in some grungy-looking kitchen. "See? They're in somebody's house, and nobody knows they're there."

"*I* know. Anyone who is watching this broadcast knows."

"Well, sure."

"Then it is hardly a secret. I am given to understand that millions of people watch these broadcasts."

"They do, but—"

"Then how can it be a secret?"

I didn't say anything for a few seconds. I wished Kathy were here. Maybe *she* could make sense out of the question. "It's a secret *in the movie*," I said finally.

"'Movie'? That word does not translate."

"You don't know what a movie is?"

"No. Please explain."

"It's just a story," I said. "It's not real."

"Not real? In what way is it 'not real'?"

"It never really happened. It's just—"

"But I see the pictures. Those are real beings, are they not?"

"Sure, but they're actors."

"'Actors'?" The suit was silent another couple of seconds. "That word does not translate suitably either. What is an 'actor'?"

"Someone who acts. Someone who—who pretends he's someone else."

Another silence, and then: "Why would someone pretend he was someone else?"

"They get paid a lot of money for it, for one thing."

"You pay people to 'act'?"

"Sure, all the time."

"And these things they do when they 'act'—these are things that other beings have already done?"

"Sometimes," I said, "like in biographies. But most of the time, it's just a story."

"A story? That is an account of something that has happened before?"

"No, a *story*. A made-up story. You know—*fiction*."

"I do not understand. These stories you speak of are not the truth?"

"Of course not. They're just *stories!*"

"They are lies, then?"

"I never thought of it like that, but I suppose you could say that."

"And these people, these 'actors,' are paid to 'act'?"

"Sure. And so are the people who write the stories for them to act in."

The suit was silent for ten or fifteen seconds, looking

first at me, then at the TV set, still flickering away, and then at me again, and the ring.

"You *pay* someone to *lie* to you?" he said finally.

"I guess you could say it like that, but it's not really lying. I mean, everyone knows that—"

But the suit wasn't listening anymore. With one last look at the TV set, he turned and walked away.

A couple seconds later, Kathy was skidding to a stop next to me and grabbing my arm.

"Well?" she said.

"You were right," I said, feeling shaky. "They *are* from outer space."

· 7 ·

"Arguing with People from Outer Space is Scary Work."

For a minute, she thought I was just making fun of her, but then I told her about the questions the suit had asked and how he didn't seem to even know what movies were and how he'd kept talking about "beings."

When she realized I *wasn't* kidding, she got this huge grin, and I thought for a second she was going to let out some kind of yell, even louder than the one she'd let go with when she'd decided they were from UFOs.

But then she got herself under control. She's good at that.

"But who *are* they?" she asked. "What are they *doing* here?"

I shook my head. "All he did was ask those dumb

questions. Whenever I tried to ask *him* something, he just ignored me."

"Next time, make a bargain with him. Tell him you won't answer *his* questions unless *he* answers *yours*."

"Next time? Look, Kathy, whatever's going on, we're getting in way over our heads. Now that we're sure these people really *are* from outer space, we better tell someone."

"Tell who? Who's going to believe us?"

"We can show them the ring."

"Sure, and they'll take it away and it won't work for them and that'll be the end of that. We'll *never* find out who they are or why they're here. Or where that ring came from or why you got it or anything."

And she was right. Or at least I'd thought the same sort of things myself, when I'd been trying to talk myself into telling Dad or Mom about the ring and the cat and everything. I mean, if I was *really* as logical as I'm supposed to be, then the first thing I would've done was show Dad the ring, and he could've taken it somewhere to have it analyzed, and it wouldn't make any difference to me that I'd never see it again or find out what it really was or anything like that. After all, logically, I'd be better off going along as usual without all this nonsense, and if the ring really *was* from outer space and detected aliens or whatever, then someone from the government *should* be handling it instead of a couple of not-quite-twelve-year-olds. That's what governments are for, sort of.

Anyway, we didn't tell anyone.

And an hour or so later, my finger started tingling again. This time we ended up on the south side of the courthouse square, where Morton Hunsacker was making a campaign speech. Morton Hunsacker is running for Congress this year, and Dad says he's "even worse than that dodo bird we elected *last* time."

We hadn't been there more than a minute or two when we saw another black suit, so much like the others we couldn't tell whether it was one we'd seen before or not.

"Don't forget," Kathy said as she shoved me toward the suit. "Don't tell him *anything* until he tells you who he is and what he's doing here. And how many of them there are."

As I came up to the suit, he was looking around, like he was expecting someone. When he saw me—and the ring—he drifted a few yards away from the crowd to meet me.

"I understand this is part of the process by which you select your leaders," the suit said. "Is that correct?"

"Yes, but—"

"Who is this other being he is accusing of such terrible crimes? Is he a leader of a group you are at war with?"

"No, we're not at war with anyone that I know of, at least not officially. It's just—"

"Then who is this other being this one is speaking about?"

"He's the congressman—the leader—this one is running against. But who—"

"This being he is attacking is one of *your* group's leaders? But if he is as evil as this being says, how did he become a leader?"

"He was elected. Now who—"

"But if he is so evil, how could he be elected?"

"He isn't *really* evil. At least I don't think so. Who—"

"This man is lying, then?"

I pulled in my breath and braced myself. "I can't answer any more of your questions until *you* answer *mine!*" I said in a rush, all in one breath.

The suit didn't say anything for a few seconds, like he was shook up by what I said, but his expression, what there was of it, didn't change.

"Is this man lying?" the suit asked again, in a louder voice, like he thought I hadn't heard him before.

"Who are you?" I asked, raising my own voice a smidgin. "Why have you come to Earth?"

Another short silence, and then: "You are *required* to answer my questions."

"I will, if you'll tell me who you are and why you're here." My heart was pounding even more than before. Arguing with people from outer space is scary work.

The suit's expression still didn't change, but I got the feeling that he was looking at me even harder than before. "Have you not been given all the information you require?"

"I haven't been given *any* information."

"But you possess the milorganite device, and you responded to my call."

"This ring? Is that the—what did you call it?"

"That is the milorganite device on your finger, yes. Were matters not explained to your satisfaction when it was given to you?"

"It *wasn't* given to me. I found it."

"Found? Then you are not one of—"

It was like the suit just shut down all of a sudden. Without another word or a change in expression or anything, he turned and ducked into the crowd. A second later, the tingle and all the rest faded away, and I couldn't see him anywhere in the crowd.

Kathy was pounding on my arm about three seconds later.

"Well?" she said, practically hopping up and down. "Who are they? What do they want?"

"He wouldn't tell me."

"Calvin Willeford! I told you to—"

"I did. I refused to answer any more questions until he answered *my* questions."

"So what happened?"

"The second he found out I didn't already know who he was, he ran away like the others," I said, and then tried to tell Kathy what had happened.

"They know all about your ring, then," she said when I more or less finished.

"I guess so. He called it a—a 'milorganite device' or something weird-sounding like that. And he said something about me 'responding to his call.'"

"So *that's* it!" Kathy said with a huge grin, like she'd all of a sudden figured out the secret of life, or at least the secret of getting good grades without studying. "It's not an alien detector, it's an outer space beeper!"

"Beeper?"

"You know, like doctors carry around. Only instead of beeping, this one makes your finger tingle. And instead of giving you a phone number to call, it hooks right into your head and tells you where to go!"

I thought about it a second or two and decided I'd liked it better when it was an alien detector instead of a Calvin caller.

"Whatever it is," I said, "I'm not supposed to have it. And now that they know I *do* have it, they'll take it back. And once they get it back, they'll have to cover the whole thing up so no one will ever find out about them, and they'll probably—"

"Calvin, come on! Calm down! You sound like you thought they were dangerous or something."

"If they're here secretly and don't want anyone to know about them, and I—*we're* the only ones who know about them, why *shouldn't* they be dangerous?"

"Why *should* they be? They haven't threatened us or acted dangerous or anything like that. I mean, four of them ran away before you had a chance to even talk to them, and one ran away as soon as you started asking questions. If you ask me, they're more scared of us than we are of them."

"More scared than *you* are, maybe. But if they all get together and decide to come after us—"

"Then maybe at least *one* of them will answer our questions!" Kathy said, and from the way she said it and from the look on her face, I could tell there wasn't any use arguing with her.

Besides, I didn't *really* want to. Argue, that is. I probably wanted to find out who they were just as badly as Kathy did, only I was logical enough to know that I should be a little scared, too.

Anyway, we spent the rest of Saturday—and Sunday, too—looking for more black suits and waiting for more finger tingles. The only trouble was, we didn't find any black suits—except for a dozen or so real ones at a funeral Sunday morning—and no matter how hard I tried, I couldn't get my finger to tingle, even a little bit.

By Monday, Kathy had decided the aliens must've left town or maybe just shut down my beeper by remote control now that they knew I'd gotten it by accident. And I was beginning to think—or maybe hope—that I'd just imagined the whole thing or had gotten mixed up in some really weird practical joke.

But then, at the end of the lunch hour Monday—Well, I guess you could say things changed. And it started to look like my life really *might* turn into a squashed bottle cap.

8

"What *Is* that Thing, Mr. Willeford?"

Like I said a while ago, Kathy and I go to the Vernon J. Dalhart Middle School, which is sixth through eighth grades. The school itself is one of those big old brick things almost as old as Mom and Dad put together. In fact, it used to be a high school, the one Mom went to back in prehistoric times. There's a parking lot for the teachers along one side, and out in the back there's an open space, not really big enough for a softball diamond, but big enough for Frisbees and that sort of thing. Beyond that's the Orpha Mae Partridge City Park, four or five blocks long and a couple blocks wide, but the important part—which I'll get back to later—is this ravine that runs all the way along the one side of the park. It's twenty or thirty feet deep and two or three times that wide most places, and it's all full of trees and bushes and rocks and things. It's a sort of boundary between the school and the park, but half the kids take shortcuts through it all the time, even if there aren't any bridges over it.

Anyway, I got through Monday morning okay, and I even made it through Ms. Armour's English test without falling apart too much, even if I *had* spent all weekend with Kathy looking for aliens instead of studying. Like always on Mondays, the "hot lunch" was chipped beef and some goopy-looking stuff with spinach in it that I don't think even Hulk or Mastodon would touch, but we shoveled down what we could and then went out and spent a few more minutes looking for black suits again. Even Kathy was getting ready to give up, though.

But then, just as we were coming back inside, one of the suits found *us*.

It wasn't anything at all like the other times. *This* suit came running up the steps behind us and slammed through the door and grabbed me by the shoulder when I was a dozen or so feet down the hall. He didn't look like he was worrying about anyone else seeing him or *anything*. He wasn't paying any attention to anything or anyone but me.

And then, in a low voice, practically in my ear, he said, "You must help me!"

Then he started to pull at me, practically dragging me back toward the door.

This time I didn't feel any finger tingle. I just felt total panic. I jerked free and jumped back a yard or two.

For a couple of seconds, the suit just stood there, and

then he took a step toward me, a gliding sort of step, almost like he was skating instead of walking. He didn't grab me again, but he leaned down toward me, and I could all of a sudden see that his face wasn't in a shadow like I'd thought it was. It was just plain blurry, like the ring had been at first.

"There's something wrong with your face," I said when I couldn't think of anything else.

The suit twitched and one hand darted inside his jacket. Then his face cleared up. Literally. It was just like those werewolf movies where Lon Chaney or somebody grows a hairy face and fangs and a wet nose right before your eyes. Only this guy just grew a face, a plain old everyday face, just like Mr. Johnson's except that it looked sort of grayish, even the lips.

I think I said, "That's better," like Mom does sometimes when she's helped Dad straighten his tie or something like that. I'm not too sure, though, because that's when he leaned even closer and said the same thing again. "You must help me! You must come with me!"

And that's also when I noticed his voice wasn't working much better than his face had been, and I don't mean just the fact that the words that came out didn't quite fit the way his lips moved. After talking to those two suits Saturday, I was almost used to that sort of thing.

This one's voice was full of *holes!* It was sort of like he had a loose wire on his speaker, and it wasn't making contact all the time.

But then, to add to the confusion, Kathy dropped her oar in the water, so to speak.

71

"We'll help you," she said, "if you'll tell us who you are and what you're here for."

The suit turned to look at her, and I was sure he was getting ready to run away, just like the others, but he didn't. He just repeated, "You must help me!"

"We will," I heard myself saying, practically repeating what Kathy had said, "as soon as you tell us who you are and why you're here on Earth."

The non-expression on the suit's face still didn't change, but he must've been getting more panicky by the second. For one thing, the hallway we were standing in was getting really jammed with all the kids coming back from lunch. There must've been fifty or sixty at least, all wandering up and down the hall and talking and laughing. And looking at the suit.

I mean, who wouldn't be looking at it? The Vernon J. Dalhart Middle School isn't like your big-city schools where the halls are patrolled by security guards with bulletproof vests and where anyone who can't prove he's a student or a teacher gets frisked and handcuffed just on general principles, but some guy in a black suit and hat with a grayish face that's starting to get fuzzy around the edges is going to attract some attention.

Anyway, I guess it was just natural that Mr. Ames, the vice-principal, would pick right then to come out of his office a few yards down the hall. He stood looking around the way he does when he's trying to find some rules being broken, and after a few seconds his eyes locked onto the suit and he headed straight for us. Kathy saw him, too, and she grabbed at the suit's arm like she was going to lead him away somewhere, but it didn't work.

It *looked* like she got a handful of jacket sleeve, but her fingers went right through, like it was all an optical illusion, with nothing really there at all. Her fingers actually disappeared inside the sleeve for a second.

She squeaked a little and jerked her hand back.

"Oh, dear," the suit said, "*that* isn't working properly either!"

At which point Mr. Ames was on top of us.

"Mr. Willeford, Ms. Entsminger," he said, using our last names in that "you're-in-deep-trouble" tone he's so good with, "would you care to introduce me to your friend?"

Kathy looked like she was still in shock from having her hand disappear inside the suit's arm, and all *I* could think of was what Mom had called the first suit back there in Bjornsen's parking lot.

"His name's Johnson," I said.

"Mr. Johnson? My name is Ames, Norbert Ames," Mr. Ames said, and he stuck his hand out to shake the suit's. "I am vice-principal here at Dalhart."

After what happened when Kathy had tried to grab the suit's sleeve, it wasn't a real big surprise when the suit didn't stick his own hand out. Ames waited a couple of seconds and then lowered his own with a sort of shrug.

"And what can we do for you, Mr. Johnson?" he asked.

"Johnson," of course, didn't say anything. Then he started to back away, which just made things worse. Mr. Ames, after a quick frown at Kathy and me, started looking *really* suspicious.

73

"Mr. Johnson," Mr. Ames said, "I do not mean to be rude, but I must insist that you state your business."

"It's all right," Kathy said, stepping up next to the suit. Apparently she'd recovered from her disappearing hand. "Calvin dropped something while we were outside just now, and Mr. Johnson found it, that's all."

Mr. Ames hesitated, looking at the suit and then at me. He still looked suspicious, and I couldn't blame him. Half the kids in the hall were watching us now.

"And just what was it you dropped, Mr. Willeford?"

Which stumped me, of course. All I could do was look at Kathy and hope she'd had something in mind when she said what she said.

But, as it turned out, it didn't matter. Neither one of us had to answer.

Because that's when the suit disappeared.

Just like the generic cat, he disappeared. One second he was there, and the next second he wasn't.

And then he was back. Only he wasn't wearing a black suit and hat anymore.

And he wasn't human.

He wasn't even *close*. He was eight or nine feet tall, or maybe ten or twelve.

And he was hairy, *really* hairy. All over. He looked kind of like the Wookiee from *Star Wars*, only he was all gray and a lot bigger and uglier, like somebody had crossed the Wookiee with an Abominable Snowman or something.

Somewhere in the hair, there was a pair of eyes, and he glanced down at himself and said, "Oh, dear!" and then let out with a noise that sounded like a cross between a Swiss yodel and a gargle, only very low-pitched, like the bass in a barbershop quartet.

If he hadn't been the center of attention before, he certainly was now.

For a couple of seconds, there wasn't a sound anywhere in the hall except for a few books and candy bars and stuff hitting the floor when people dropped them. Even Mr. Ames didn't say anything. His jaw just dropped down till you couldn't see the knot in his tie, and his eyes—well, I guess they didn't actually pop out of his head, but they sure looked like they were trying.

Then the big, hairy thing moved. It took a shuffling step toward me.

At which point, everybody got his or her voice back, and it was all of a sudden like we were in the middle of a rock concert audience, with everyone yelling and screaming at the top of their lungs.

Except for Mr. Ames. He recovered enough to edge a few inches closer to me and say, "What *is* that thing, Mr. Willeford?" From the way he said it, I could tell that, no matter what the "thing" turned out to be, he was already convinced that it was my fault.

I almost said, "That's what we were trying to find out before you scared it," but I didn't. Or I don't think I did. The difference between what was real and what wasn't was getting sort of shaky.

Anyway, whether I said anything or not, that's when the thing, the ex-suit, turned and ran. That of course set off a lot of new screaming from the three or four dozen kids watching, but even with all the noise, I could still hear its big feet thumping on the floor.

75

Kathy grabbed my arm, like she'd tried to grab the suit's before. Only with me, it worked.

"Come on!" she yelled over all the other yelling. "Don't let it get away!"

And believe it or not, I went. No second thoughts or even any first thoughts. I just ran, even getting a few feet ahead of Kathy now and then. The mass of other kids in the hall didn't slow us up, not with that thing in front of us. They scattered like crazy, tripping over each other and jumping through doors and trying to climb the wall-mounted fire hoses, anything to get out of the way.

Then the thing was bending practically double to get through the eight-foot doors to the outside, and we were pounding along after it. Another fifty or a hundred kids and a couple of teachers were outside, and they scattered pretty much the same way the ones on the inside had done, only these had more room to scatter in. Some in the parking lot jumped on top of cars, and a couple even crawled underneath, and out in the back, one of the kids that had been tossing a Frisbee around just stood and stared while it bounced off his head. But what he was staring at was the ex-suit, not us. I don't think anyone even *saw* the two of us galloping along behind.

Then the ex-suit was at the edge of the ravine, and without even hesitating, he was over the edge and sliding down out of sight. Kathy and I got to the edge a few seconds later and went down about as fast as he had. With all the bushes and trees and things down there, we couldn't see him, but we could still hear him.

For a few seconds, anyway. Then, all of a sudden, the noise stopped, except for what we were making ourselves.

And except for all the yells and "What-was-that's" and just plain screams from up in the school yard.

We stopped and listened, but it didn't do any good. There was still nothing making noise down in the ravine except us, and after a few seconds, Kathy started pushing through the bushes and things in more or less the direction of the last sound we'd heard from the ex-suit.

But there was nothing there, at least nothing big and hairy, which was all we were really interested in. There were trees growing out of the sides of the ravine, and bushes were everywhere, and what maybe used to be a creek bed a couple feet wide right in the middle, only now it was mostly dried up except for a few damp spots. And every so often there were some big rocks, like boulders, sticking out of the ground. Most of them had arrows and hearts and initials and a bunch of dirty words carved in them or spray-painted on them.

But not a thing to tell us where the ex-suit had disappeared to.

"What does your finger have to say?" Kathy asked.

"Not a thing. It wasn't working even when that thing was right *next* to me. Besides, are you sure you really *want* to find it?"

She gave me a look like I'd just gone off the rails altogether. "Don't tell me *you don't!*"

"Well, sure I do, but we better get back to school before they miss us," I said. "Mr. Ames is probably going to blame us for the whole thing anyway."

"I suppose you're right," she said, but she didn't sound like she really meant it. She looked around again. "But how'd that thing disappear like that? For that matter, how'd those other two disappear the way they did in that alley next to the jail?"

I shrugged. "Maybe they really *do* disappear. For just a second there, it *looked* like he turned invisible or something, just like that cat."

She poked at the air a few times, then shook her head. "Maybe he looks like something *else* now." She reached out and tapped a tree with her finger.

I just watched. If that thing really *was* disguised as a tree or something, I didn't think I wanted to try sticking my finger into it.

"Come on," I said, starting back to where we'd slid down into the ravine. "We better get back."

I'd gone only eight or ten feet, though, before I saw something.

A footprint.

It was right in the middle of the ravine, in one of the muddy spots. It was at least eighteen or twenty inches long. And it had seven toes.

The next thing I knew, Kathy was looking over my shoulder, all excited again.

"He *did* go this way!" she said, looking off through the bushes in the direction the footprint was pointing.

"If his toes are on the front of his feet," I said.

She snorted. "It'd be just like you to find the first monster from outer space with his feet on backwards. Now come on. Maybe we can still find it."

Like you might guess, I followed.

But not very far. Ten or twelve yards along, I almost bumped into Kathy, she stopped so suddenly.

78

"Calvin!" she said, trying to yell and whisper at the same time. "This rock doesn't belong here!"

She was standing next to a big, gray rock, sort of a boulder five or six feet high, like you see along the side of the trail in western movies. It looked like it was sunk another couple of feet into the ground, and into the side of the ravine, too.

"Are you sure?" I asked. I didn't remember ever seeing it before, but I don't know exactly where every rock in the park is.

"Just look at it!" she said.

So I looked. And after a second, I saw what she meant. There wasn't a single heart or date or name, not even a dirty word, carved or painted on it, and the whole surface had the same sort of smooth, gray look the suit's face had had.

And while I looked, I could see she was working up the nerve to poke at it with her finger, the way she had with the tree.

Finally, she did. Holding her arm way out in front of her, like she was getting ready to stick her finger in a can of worms, she poked at the rock.

And her finger disappeared.

It went right inside the rock, along with most of her hand.

She jerked her hand back, but before either of us could do anything but blink, a pair of very large, very hairy arms reached out of the rock and grabbed *our* arms and practically yanked us off our feet.

9

"You *Lost* Your Whole *Ship?*"

All I had time to do was think, "Now we've *really* done it!" Then we were inside the rock.
That's right, *inside the rock!*

Only of course it wasn't a rock, any more than the suit had been a suit. It just looked like one from the outside. From the inside, it didn't look like much of anything, since it was almost pitch black. The rock, or whatever it really was, was sort of like a one-way mirror. When we were outside, we hadn't been able to see inside, but now that we were inside, we could see outside just fine. But we still couidn't see much of what was inside, mainly because it was so dark in there.

Not that I was thinking any of this right then. I wasn't thinking much of anything, except maybe wishing I was in Outer Mongolia or someplace nice and safe like that.

But then I heard the suit's voice again. It was as full of

holes as the last time I'd heard it, but at least it wasn't that gargling bass yodel we'd heard back in the Dalhart hallway.

And it was still saying the same thing. "You must help me!"

Which was, under the circumstances, something of a relief. A lot better than, say, "Hold still or I'll vaporize you."

But then, before I could say, "Whatever you want," Kathy said:

"Will you tell us who you are and why you're here?"

As you can see, it takes a lot to shake Kathy up enough to sidetrack her. When she decides she wants something, she really sticks with it.

There was a long silence—or at least there in the dark with those hairy hands on us, it seemed like a long one. Finally the voice said, "If I tell you what you want to know, will you then help me?"

"Yes!" we chorused.

After another silence—this one lasted only a month or two—the voice said, "Very well. I have no choice."

And the hairy hands let us go.

I surprised myself by not jumping back outside the rock the second I had the chance. Finally, my eyes got used to the dark, and I could see that it wasn't completely dark after all. It was like I was standing in a very deep shadow, with light all around me, only there wasn't anything to cause the shadow. It must've been the "rock," but from the inside, I couldn't see it.

Anyway, there was enough light inside there to see that the ex-suit was as big and hairy as the last time we'd seen him. He was squatting on the ground so he could fit inside the rock, but even squatting, his head was a couple feet above ours.

"Where are you from?" Kathy asked.

Some of the hair where his mouth should've been moved, but no sound came out, like he forgot to turn the volume up.

"What's wrong?" Kathy asked.

"Oh, dear. I was afraid that might happen." The hair moved again, but the words didn't even come close to matching the movements. And behind the words, I thought I could hear a really faint version of that gargling yodel he'd nailed everyone to the wall with back in the hallway. And that *did* sort of match the way the hair moved.

"Afraid *what* would happen?" Kathy asked.

"Names cannot be translated."

"What names?"

"Any names. The name of the world I am from."

"Just tell us where it is, then," Kathy said.

The hairy face looked up, toward the sky. "It is up there somewhere."

"Terrific!" Kathy said, but I don't think the ex-suit caught the sarcasm, since the next thing he said was:

"Thank you."

Kathy sort of rolled her eyes like she couldn't believe what she was hearing. "You're from another solar system, is that it? Another star?"

"Yes. A planet in another stellar system."

"How far away is it?"

"I don't know."

"You don't *know?* Which direction is it in, then?"

"I don't know."

"If you don't know how far away it is or which way it is, how are you going to find your way back?"

"My ship will take me."

"Your *ship* knows where you're from, but *you* don't?"

"Of course."

"Will your *ship* tell us where you're from?"

"It can show you."

"Well, that's a start, I guess. Where's your ship?"

"I don't know. That is why I need your help! I am unable to locate my ship!"

"You *lost* your whole *ship?*"

"That did not translate."

"*Why* can't you locate your ship?"

"Because my equipment is not functioning properly."

"What equipment?"

"The equipment that locates my ship."

"Something that points to it, you mean? Like a compass?"

A silence, and then, "That is essentially correct."

"Is that all you need us for?" I asked when Kathy sort of ran down, or maybe ran out of breath. "To help you find your ship?"

"Yes. You must find it and take me to it."

"*Take* you to it? Looking like this?" I had real trouble imagining us leading either a ten-foot hairy monster or a six-foot boulder through the streets of East Gradwohl. Or anywhere else, for that matter.

"We could take him later," Kathy said, grabbing hold of my arm. "After dark or something like that."

"Maybe," I said. "*If* we can find his ship. I mean, if *he* can't find it, what makes you think *we* can? We don't even know what it looks like or where he left it or anything! We—"

"We must be silent now," the ex-suit said, and all of a sudden, his hands were holding our arms like a couple of big, hairy vises.

10

"You Are Interesting
and You Do Not
Cost Much."

"What—" I began, but before I could say anything else, I saw what he was talking about.
And heard it.

A couple of eighth-graders had come down into the
ravine, and two or three dozen others were lined up along
the edge, looking down after them.

The two were just sort of looking around, like Kathy
and I'd done at first, only they looked more nervous, like
maybe someone had dared them to come down. Which
someone probably had. They're always doing illogical
things like that.

"Can they hear us?" I whispered.

"I was told that sound is unable to escape from this
place," the ex-suit said in what I guess was his version of a

whisper, "but I was also told that my equipment could not malfunction."

"We better be pretty quiet, then," Kathy said.

And we were. Or at least we tried. When they were right next to the rock, I even tried to breathe quietly, but I just ended up breathing slowly, not quietly, and after a minute or so I was out of breath and making more noise than before. But they didn't seem to notice, so I guess whatever it was that was supposed to keep the sound from getting out of the rock must've been working after all.

Anyway, neither of them gave the rock a second look, and then they found the footprint. They just sort of stared for a couple of seconds, and then they started looking all around, real fast, like they were expecting whatever'd made the footprint to jump on them out of nowhere.

Which the ex-suit could've done, but he didn't, of course.

And that's when Sheriff Pippenger showed up. I suppose Mr. Ames must've called him.

Anyway, he was up on the edge of the ravine looking down, looking right at the two eighth-graders.

"All right, you kids down there!" he yelled. "Whatever you're doing, you can stop it right this minute!"

For a couple of seconds, they froze. Pippenger affects people that way. But then, when he started down into the ravine, slipping and sliding down the side, they started talking—both at the same time, of course—and pointing, mostly at the footprint.

Pippenger looked sort of mussed by the time he got to the bottom and pushed through all the bushes and things, and there were smudges all over his tan uniform.

He also looked annoyed, even more than he usually did, and the way he *usually* looked was enough to back you into a corner at thirty paces.

Then he saw the footprint, and you could just see him tighten up even more, like somebody was turning a screw inside him.

He stood looking down at the footprint, and while he did, the two kids didn't make a sound. Then he looked up at them.

"I suppose you're going to tell me that thing you all saw back there in school made this—this footprint." He wasn't asking them, he was accusing them.

"It must've," the one said.

"It was big enough, that's for sure!" the other said.

Pippenger kept on looking at them. "Who are you trying to kid?" he asked, and his voice sounded about like his face looked. "You just got through *making* this thing! *Didn't you?*"

"No!" one of them said, and the other just looked at the ground, like he wished he could crawl into it and disappear.

"Don't kid a kidder!" Pippenger said, whatever that meant. "Just tell me where that friend of yours in the bear suit got to!"

Now they both just looked blank, and Pippenger looked back at the footprint.

"I suppose you think I'm going to fall for this!" he said. "Well, you've got another think coming, I can tell you that!"

At which point he jammed his own foot into the footprint. "I bet you think this is real cute, don't you!" he said. His lips hardly moved at all, and he looked sort of red in the face. "Well, *this* is how cute *I* think it is!"

And he stomped the footprint until there was nothing left but a bunch of his own heelprints.

"Now let's get back up to school," he said, "and you can explain how cute you think everything is to Mr. Ames. *And* to your parents!"

And that was more or less that. Sheriff Pippenger herded the two kids back out of the ravine and handed them over to Mr. Ames, who was at the edge of the ravine now, along with three or four of the teachers. Then he chased everyone away from the ravine, and finally *he* left, and we were alone with the ex-suit again.

"You want us to find your ship for you," Kathy said, picking up right where we'd left off maybe twenty minutes before. Not a word about going back to school or anything sensible like that. But, then, I wasn't thinking much about going back either, at least not right now.

"That is correct," the ex-suit said, and I noticed that his voice was getting even more full of holes than before, like whatever was wrong with it was getting worse.

"But if *you* don't know where it is, how can *we* find it?" I asked, which was pretty much what I'd asked before Pippenger showed up. I still hadn't thought of an answer. "And even if we *could* find it, how could we take you there? I mean, unless you can start looking human again—"

"I cannot."

"What happened?" Kathy asked. "You looked sort of weird before, but at least you looked human."

"The equipment that maintains my image is no longer functioning properly."

"Maintains your image?"

"The image that you saw is generated so that I may move among you without attracting attention. But my equipment is no longer able to generate that image."

"Then this is really you?" Kathy asked. "You really *are* a ten-foot hairy monster? This isn't just another—another image?"

"That did not translate entirely. But this is what I look like. It is not an image."

"And this rock, or whatever it is?" I said. "This thing we're inside of—how did you do *that?*"

"It is another image. It is for emergency use only. It is simple to generate and maintain. The other image must be able to follow my movements, but this one does not have to move."

"Like a slide projector instead of a movie projector," Kathy said helpfully.

"But even it is not working properly," the ex-suit said. "It is supposed to generate a field of force that matches the image."

"So it would feel solid, you mean? So I couldn't stick my finger through it?"

"That is essentially correct."

"But anyway," Kathy said, "you can't make yourself look like something else? Something that wouldn't attract so much attention?"

"I cannot."

"Then Calvin's right. Even if we *can* find this ship of yours—"

"You will have to bring it to me, then," the ex-suit said.

Neither one of us said anything for a few seconds. "Fly it, you mean?" Kathy finally said, sounding like she was getting ready to open a Christmas present from some millionaire aunt.

"That is correct."

"You want *us* to pilot an interstellar *space*ship?" I sort of squeaked, ignoring the looks Kathy was giving me.

"It is easy. If it were not easy, I could not do it myself."

"But you've had lots of training."

"I have had no training."

"But *we* can't even drive a *car* yet!" I said. The whole idea of trying to operate a spaceship, for crying out loud, sort of curdled my mind. I mean, I'd seen pictures of the control panels they used to have in those Apollo space-ships, and *they* only went to the *moon!* It'd take *years* to learn all that stuff, and here this ex-suit wanted us to fly something that could go to the *stars!* Without even a driver training class!

"I can tell you how to do it," he said. "It is very simple."

Even Kathy was starting to look a little doubtful, and *she* had learned to ride a bicycle—uphill, no less—in one afternoon.

But the ex-suit didn't seem to notice any of this. His hand disappeared inside the mass of hair somewhere around his chest, and I realized he must be wearing some kind of harness under it. Unless the whole thing was just a very hairy space suit.

Anyway, the next thing we knew, he was handing me what looked like a triangular credit card, a little piece of plastic—or something—that sort of glimmered in the dim light.

"To open the door," he said, "you touch this to a spot on the outside of the ship."

"What spot?"

"It will glow when you are near the ship."

"And then?"

"When you touch the spot, the door will open. You will go inside, and you will touch another spot to close the door. There will be another glowing spot near the front of the ship. Touch that also, and the controls will appear. Touch it again and they will be activated. There are only two controls. They—"

"Only *two*? On a *spaceship*?"

"That is all it needs. They are rods that you can grip with your hands. One controls the direction of the ship. The other controls its speed. It is very easy. You will see."

I still had trouble believing it could really be that easy, but Kathy didn't seem to have any doubts anymore. She was looking at the little triangular card—the "key" to the spaceship, I guess it was—as I stuffed it in my pocket, and her mouth was almost watering.

"Okay," I said, "I guess I'll have to take your word for it. But how do we find your ship in the first place? You said you didn't know where it was."

Well, to cut a long story short, it turned out after

another forty or fifty questions that he remembered what the place where he left the ship *looked* like. He just didn't have any idea where the place was. And he had trouble describing the place, too, or at least the gadget that did his translations had some trouble.

But finally we figured out that the place he was describing was Harry's Junkyard, which was one of the landmarks of East Gradwohl. Or one of the eyesores, depending on who you talked to. Anyway, Kathy and I both knew where it was, way out on the northeast edge of town, just outside the city limits.

As for finding the spaceship itself, that was going to be a little harder, mainly because it didn't look like a ship, any more than the suit had looked like a monster at first. It had "disguised" itself more or less the same way. Unless, of course, *its* equipment had conked out, too.

Anyway, to attract as little attention as possible, the ship normally made itself look like whatever it was next to, which meant it was probably just one more rusty car in the middle of hundreds of other rusty cars, or maybe thousands. Harry's is a pretty big junkyard, and he's got stuff from all over three or four counties. The only thing that looked like it might make it a little easier for us was that the spot where we were supposed to stick the "key" would start glowing when we got close to it, maybe eight or ten feet away.

By the time we got all this sorted out, I was ready to head for Harry's, but Kathy had other ideas. She still wanted to find out who the ex-suit really was and what he was doing here and who all the other suits were and just about anything else she could think of.

So naturally she started asking questions all over again, and this time she got a few answers. Quite a few, in fact.

Not that it was easy. For one thing, about the time we figured out that the missing spaceship was stashed in Harry's Junkyard, the ravine turned into a sort of East Gradwohl Grand Central Station. First, Jeff Cantwell and a couple others from the *East Gradwohl Gazette* showed up to look around and take pictures while Mr. Ames and Sheriff Pippenger stood by looking grim. Then someone from the TV station over in Cranston showed up and took some more pictures, especially of Mr. Ames up at the top of the ravine. (Sheriff Pippenger stayed out of sight.) There were even a bunch of the kids around by then, including the ones who'd watched Pippenger stomp out the footprint.

Anyway, that sort of stuff kept happening off and on for the next couple of hours, and in between times, Kathy and I—mostly Kathy—grilled the ex-suit. Which, like I said, wasn't easy. Half of her questions couldn't be translated by the ex-suit's gadget, and half of what did get translated, he couldn't understand. And half of his answers didn't make a lot of sense either, but then, about the time the guys from the TV station left, something must've clicked in Kathy's head, sort of like it had when she'd connected the black suits with that old UFO writer, Barker or whatever his name was.

The way it happened was, after we finally figured out that this was this particular suit's first visit to Earth but that others had been coming here for hundreds of years, I came right out and asked one of my dumber questions:

"Are you invading us?" It seemed logical at the time, even if Kathy did give me a dirty look.

"Invading?" the ex-suit asked. "I do not understand."

"You know," I said, "conquering us and using us for slaves or food or something like that."

His hair gave a really big ripple, kind of like wind blowing through a field of tall grass. "Of course not! We are civilized!"

"Then why *are* you here?"

"You are interesting and you do not cost much."

And that's when the light bulb came on in Kathy's head. Later, she told me it was all so logical I should've come up with it myself. There were the weird questions those other suits had asked me, and there was the way they "disguised" themselves so they could "move among" us without attracting attention. And there was the way they ran off whenever anyone looked at them the wrong way.

So naturally, something in her head put it all together and came up with the right answer. They weren't invaders. They were tourists! What else?

11

"What You Might Call 'Native Guides.'"

After that, we got pretty much the whole story, or at least as much of it as the ex-suit knew, which sometimes wasn't all that much. Which shouldn't have surprised us, considering he didn't even know where his home planet was.

Anyway, it turned out that Kathy was right about them being tourists, even if "tourist" wasn't one of the words that the translator could handle. What he did say was that he and the other suits were "travelers who are interested in the quaint practices of the inhabitants of backward worlds," which included Earth as far as they were concerned. "Backward," I guess, means that we don't know how to hop from star to star and all that sort of thing.

The suits weren't all from the same planet, by the way. There are hundreds, or maybe thousands, of "advanced worlds" out there all over our galaxy and maybe a few others, with all sorts of different races. He didn't really know how many there were, any more than I'd know how many individual families there might be on Earth. He didn't even know where the worlds were, not even his own. All he knew was that lots of people, including himself, took vacations and traveled, just like humans.

Only they traveled a lot farther.

They also used the alien equivalent of travel agencies, including some real cheapies. They rented ships from these agencies, sort of like we rent cars from Hertz and Avis, only these ships could be programed like a computer to take you to any bunch of worlds you wanted, including lots of "backward" ones like Earth, where the people didn't even know all these other worlds and races existed. You didn't even have to know where any of the worlds were. You just picked them out of a catalog and let the travel agent punch them into the ship's computer. The ship took you to them, one after the other, and brought you back.

Provided you didn't lose the ship, of course.

And provided the gadget that kept you looking and sounding more or less human didn't spring a leak, like his had.

As for the ring—the "milorganite device"—Kathy had been right again, at least on her second guess. It *was* a sort of outer space beeper that hooked right into your head.

Normally, according to the ex-suit, the only people

who wear those rings are what you might call "native guides." And it looks like that's what I almost was. It's what I probably *would* have been if this cheapie agency's local representative hadn't gotten in a fight with Hulk and if I hadn't doused him with a glass of water. I guess he'd been following me around a few days, listening to me or checking out what I read—mostly science fiction, by the way—and he'd probably decided I was "suitable" for the job and was getting ready to "interview" me for it.

According to the ex-suit, anyway, that's how the local representatives for these cut-rate outfits usually worked. The only trouble was, this one had run into Hulk and the water, which I guess fouled up his own equipment, so his cat disguise disappeared and he dropped the ring.

And I found it, and then all the tourists who happened to be in the neighborhood started paging me, only whenever Kathy or my brother or any other "unauthorized" person started paying too much attention to them, they ran.

The bigger agencies didn't operate like that, of course. They gave you a full-fledged guided tour, like those "six-countries-in-six-weeks" European tours that Aunt Gladys is always taking. The guides aren't natives, and there's always one of them with you to make sure you don't get lost or order the wrong food or insult the mayor or something.

And these bigger agencies also usually gave you an image maker that could make you look like something besides a rock or a black suit. Or invisible, which, by the way, is how all those suits kept getting away from us. They just disappeared, literally. The only trouble was, they couldn't stay that way for long, mainly because it made them blind and deaf to everything around them, and they'd be pretty sure to bump into something—or someone—if they tried to move around very much. About all they could do was duck behind a tree or something, disappear, and hope that nobody tripped over them. Or saw them when they reappeared.

But these other outfits— Well, from what the ex-suit said, taking a vacation with one of them would be sort of like renting a camper and a gorilla suit and going out to live with the apes for a few days, with maybe one or two of the apes able to answer your questions.

Only this particular vacationer couldn't find his camper. And his gorilla suit was coming apart at the seams.

As for why there had been so many suits asking me questions all of a sudden, that was about the only question he actually *knew* the answer to. This one agency, the one he'd rented his camper and gorilla suit from, also ran what amounted to tour buses, which were just like the campers except they held a couple dozen tourists and were even cheaper. He'd been on one of those a few years before, to a whole different set of worlds, and it'd driven him buggy, having to practically take a vote every time you wanted to stay a few minutes longer or leave a world an hour ahead of schedule. And when I mentioned "Mr. Johnson" and the old Diefenbacher place, he guessed that maybe the agency was buying it so they'd have an out-of-the-way place to park their buses while everybody looked around. Which would be a lot handier than having to find a new place every time, like he'd had to find

Harry's Junkyard, where one more junked car would never be noticed.

But to get back to what had happened to *him*, he had seen me and the ring Saturday, while his gadgets had all been working the way they were supposed to. In fact, he'd been the one watching the wedding. Saturday night, then, he'd decided he was ready to move on to the next world on his list, but when he started to go back to his ship, he found out that the gadget that was supposed to lead him to it wasn't working. And neither was the gadget that was supposed to call up a native guide.

Needless to say, he panicked. Ever since then, he'd been wandering around town, hoping he'd stumble onto his ship or at least onto a guide who could show him where it was. He'd been getting desperate enough to start talking to "unauthorized natives" by the time he finally spotted me and came charging into the Dalhart hallway after me.

And then his disguise gadget broke down like everything else, and he panicked even worse. And ran. It was just good luck, I guess, that we followed him.

By the time we'd gotten all this information out of him, it was almost like we were old friends, and the fact that he was ten feet tall and hairy and from a planet a few thousand light years away didn't much bother me. Or Kathy, although I'm not so sure that all that stuff had bothered her even at the start. Even the fact that the whole world might be knee deep in aliens didn't scare me anymore. After all, if what he said was true, it had been that way for the last few thousand years, and nobody'd ever even noticed.

But then, just when we were getting ready to go back out into the real world, and we were telling him how we would probably have to wait until after dark to bring his ship to him, even if we *were* able to find it, his voice suddenly developed a whole new batch of holes. And he sort of twitched all over, like he'd been poked in the stomach or something.

"Oh, dear," he said, or at least that's what it sounded like, but what with the holes, it was hard to tell. And at the same time, his hair all stood on end for a second, like it does in those static electricity experiments.

"Oh, dear," he said again. "I do not know if I can survive that long."

"What's wrong?" I asked. "Did something happen?"

"Another piece of equipment has failed," he said, but it took him three times to say it so we could understand him. "It is the one that allows me to breathe your atmosphere."

"But you're still breathing," Kathy said. "Aren't you?"

"There is another system that will sustain me for a short time, a few of your hours, but it will not last for long. It is only for emergencies, like this image I am forced to use."

"A few hours?" All of a sudden I felt sick, really sick, like I was going to throw up. I'd felt the same way once when Dad and I'd found Murphy stretched out under the back porch, and we'd had to take him to the vet, and they'd had to—

I swallowed real hard, and a little of the feeling went away. "How many hours?" I asked.

"I do not know precisely," he said. "Certainly no more than ten."

That would make it around midnight.

So we had until midnight to find his ship.

And bring it back.

If we didn't make it . . .

· 12 ·

"What Else Could There Be?"

L uckily, by this time things had quieted down in the
ravine. Nobody'd been down there to take pictures
or anything else for almost half an hour, so at least
we didn't have any trouble getting out of the rock without
being seen.

And *we'd* quieted down, too, in a different sort of way.
Even Kathy didn't say much while we worked our way
down the ravine so we could come out somewhere away
from the school, and she looked pretty serious. I suppose
I did, too. I mean, it was one thing to have someone from
outer space to *talk* to and even help out, but to have his
life depending on you was more than enough to give you
the willies, particularly when you weren't all that sure
you could actually save him, no matter how easy he said
it would be.

And then, when we climbed out of the ravine on the

park side, at least two blocks from the school, and the first thing we heard was an official-sounding voice calling our names—well, it didn't look like our rescue mission was getting off to a very good start.

But it wasn't as bad as it *could* have been. At least it was Hostetler who was waiting for us to show up, not Pippenger. In fact, for a second or two, I actually thought about telling Hostetler the whole story and asking him to help.

"Sheriff *thought* there might be a few stragglers down there," he said. "A dozen or so never came back to school after all the excitement, so he wanted me to keep an eye out, just in case they were still around, maybe even puttin' together some more mischief like that footprint he told me about. I don't suppose you two were doing anything like that?"

We shook our heads and looked at the ground.

"Just cuttin' classes, is that it?" he asked.

"Sort of, I guess," Kathy admitted.

"You both know better than that, 'specially this close to the end of the term."

We just kept looking at the ground. Even Kathy was stumped for something worthwhile to say.

"I suppose," he went on, "you were lookin' for whatever it was that raised such a ruckus at school. Ames *said* you two had something to do with it, or at least you were talking to the guy when he turned into a bear, or whatever it was he turned into."

"I guess we were," I said, and I was getting closer all the time to telling him the whole truth.

"So what *is* the story? I heard a lot of different versions."

"Different versions?" Kathy asked. She was trying to sound innocent now, not that it fooled Hostetler.

He nodded. "About forty-seven, I think. One from each witness. Glowing red eyes, Mike Decker said. Bloody fangs, like something out of a bad Dracula movie, according to Jerry Peters. Don't remember who said it had four arms, but somebody did. Foot-long claws, a barbed tail and horns, you name it and somebody saw it. Somebody even said he saw some kind of Buck Rogers ray gun in one paw. So what did you two see? You must've seen something, since the only thing more than two or three people agree about is that you were right there on top of it when it did whatever it did."

So we told him what we'd seen, at least up to the point where we slid down into the ravine. I almost told him the rest, but Kathy took over about then and just said the thing had disappeared by the time we got down there, and we'd been wandering around looking ever since.

"And this 'Mr. Johnson' business? Ames said you called him Johnson. Before he turned into a monster, that is."

So we had to explain that, too, about how he looked just like the guy that Mom had sold the Diefenbacher place to last Friday. He just listened, the way he does, and you couldn't tell if he believed us or not. Since I wasn't telling any outright lies, just leaving out part of the truth, maybe my voice wasn't giving us away as much as it might've. Besides, Kathy did most of the talking. I'd start a sentence and she'd finish it, which, now that I think about it, was probably sort of suspicious all by itself.

But anyway, after ten or twenty minutes, he let us go— and told us that we didn't have to bother going back to school until morning, since it had been shut down for the afternoon. Seems there was just too much excitement for anyone to do anything but talk about the "monster," and besides, all those people from the *Gazette* and then the TV station had stirred things up so much that the teachers all just gave up and Mr. Ames more or less threw up his hands and told everyone to go home and get it out of their systems and come back tomorrow, but they had darned well better be ready to make up for all the lost time.

"So I guess you lucked out," Hostetler said.

"I guess we did," Kathy agreed.

"And there's nothing else you want to tell me?"

"What else could there be?" Kathy asked. I just kept quiet.

"Who knows? But if there *is* anything, you better let me know." He was quiet for a few seconds, just looking at us. "You really better," he added. "If you're mixed up in anything, you really better let me know. It'd be a lot better to hear it from you than from someone else, especially if it's something the sheriff'll end up hearing about anyway. You know how he is. And you know I'll put in a good word for you—if I can."

I really came close to telling him then. *Really* close.

But I didn't. He could tell I was holding out on him, I was sure, and I knew he meant well and all that, but I also knew he'd probably have to tell Pippenger whatever he found out from us, and if Pippenger found out about what was in the rock in the ravine . . .

So we practically ran home and got our bikes, and I met Kathy at Harry's. Harry—he's about seventy-five and doesn't care much for kids, or anybody else that isn't looking for something to buy or bringing in something to sell—kept an eye on us the whole time we were there, either him or his son, who helps out. Kathy made up a story about looking for a gas cap for her mother's VW, but that only lasted us about five minutes, until Harry found a squashed VW with a perfect gas cap, which he was willing to part with for practically nothing.

Anyway, it only took us a few minutes to figure out that this wasn't going to work. In the first place, we probably couldn't see the little glowing spot we were looking for in the daylight. And in the second place, even if we could, and even if we did find the ship, Harry was never going to let us mess around with it, since it would still look like one of his cars. And even if we did find it and got in it and were able to fly it like the ex-suit said . . .

My mind sort of overloaded at the thought of flying a spaceship—or a busted-up car—around East Gradwohl in broad daylight.

Our only chance, I decided—and Kathy didn't argue, for a change—was to come back after dark, when nobody was around and when nobody, I hoped, could see us flying the thing around, whatever it looked like.

So I went back home, and so did Kathy, and we agreed to meet after supper. We'd say we were going to the library or something. Our folks trusted us, so there wouldn't be any real problem, at least not then. If we didn't get back in an hour or two, then there would be a problem.

But not as big a problem as the ex-suit would have if we didn't help him, or so I told myself.

"*This* Was a *Spaceship?*"

A
nyway, like I said, I went home. The excitement
had all happened too late for anything to get in
the *Gazette* about it, but Mom had heard about
it down at Carbuncle and wanted to get all the inside
dope from me. So I pretty much repeated what Kathy and
I'd told Hostetler, only I said the thing looked more like a
Wookiee than a bear, and by that time Dad was home,
and *he* wanted to hear about it. He of course figured it
really *was* just someone dressed up in a bear suit or a
Wookiee suit or whatever. I mean, what else could it be?
A monster from outer space?

But then Hulk started acting weird. In the first place,
he wouldn't come close to me. Normally he spent half
the evening rubbing against my legs or trying to play with
my shoelaces, but all he'd do now was watch me from a
distance, or from under things or from around a corner,

and whenever I got close or tried to pick him up he'd lay his ears back and kind of slither backward. And the few times he did come anywhere near me, he just sniffed at me with his mouth open, the way he does whenever I've been messing around with some unauthorized animal, like a neighbor's cat. I suppose it was all that monster smell on me, and I wondered how Kathy was getting along with Mastodon.

And then there was Walter.

Walter looked at me kind of funny, too, but he didn't say anything, and I wondered if maybe he was able to see or smell something different about me, like Hulk. I mean, he'd acted kind of funny Friday, when I found the ring. And he'd been scared of that suit in Bjornsen's parking lot, like he knew there was something different about him.

But that was crazy, of course, thinking my kid brother had a sixth sense or anything like that.

Or at least that's what I kept telling myself, but after supper he was still watching me and making me even more nervous than everything else was already making me.

And that's when he mentioned the ring.

The ring that nobody could see unless I shoved it right under their noses and pointed at it.

"That sure is a dumb lookin' ring, Calvin," he said.

I'd been working up the nerve to ask Mom if it was okay to go down to the library to meet Kathy and work on some stuff for school, so it took me a second to shift gears. I should've taken longer.

"You can *see* it?" I said.

"Sure I can see it," he said, giving me one of his "What-kind-of-dumb-question-is-that?" looks. "What kind is it?"

"I don't know. Just a ring."

"Where'd *you* get it?"

"I found it."

And that, of course, was when Mom slipped up behind me. She'd been on the phone with somebody from Carbuncle, talking about what had happened at school, and I hadn't heard her hang up or anything.

"What did you find, Calvin?" she asked.

"Nothing," I said, which wasn't any too bright, either.

"Some dumb-lookin' ring," Walter said.

So naturally we went through almost the same sort of thing that I'd gone through with Kathy and her folks Saturday morning, only it was Walter who was pointing the ring out and starting to get mad when Mom couldn't see it right away and he thought she was making fun of him.

But she finally saw it, and she acted more like Kathy than like Mrs. Entsminger, the way she started asking questions. How had I done it, and where had I gotten the ring, and all that sort of thing.

But lucky for me, the phone rang again right about then, and it was somebody else from Carbuncle wanting to talk to her, so I was off the hook, at least for as long as she was on the phone. So before I could get trapped again, I got away from Walter and found Dad as fast as I could and told him about having to go to the library to meet Kathy and look up some stuff for school. He was always in favor of me going to the library, or doing anything else that had to do with reading, so I was out of the house before Mom got off the phone.

And before Walter could start up with Dad about the ring, which is what it looked like he was going to do any second.

Kathy, of course, was outside waiting for me, and probably the only reason she hadn't gone off by herself was that I still had the watchamacallit the ex-suit had given us to operate the ship.

The crosstown sneak itself got a little hairy a couple of times, although it was probably more because of us being nervous than anything else. I mean, normally neither one of us would duck into an alley or behind a hedge at the sight of a sheriff's department car a block away, but that's what we were both doing this evening. It made for a nervous trip, not to mention a slow one.

But we made it to Harry's Junkyard in forty-five minutes or so, maybe ten or fifteen minutes after it got completely dark. Nobody was around, and the big chain-link gate was padlocked like always, but the fence—wood, so the junked cars wouldn't spoil the view for people driving by, I guess—was only about six feet high, so we were able to haul ourselves over with only a couple of snags in our jeans.

Inside the fence it was, you'll pardon the expression, a whole different world. And to tell the truth, it was scary. A lot scarier than hanging out with the ex-suit had been. There were a couple of big lights up on twenty-foot poles, and there was an almost full moon in the east, but the whole place looked—well, like nothing we'd ever seen. And we'd both been there just a few hours before, so it wasn't that it was unfamiliar. It's just that it looked *different* at night. During the day, those rows of mashed cars just looked like rows of mashed cars. But now, with all the shadows and not a sound anywhere except what we were making ourselves, they looked—well, they looked like *dead* cars, if that makes any sense, which it probably doesn't.

And the shadows all looked like there were things in them that shouldn't be there, things that were watching us, like the ex-suit had been watching us from inside that imaginary rock of his. I even kept thinking I heard little pings and clinks coming from the rows of cars, like they were settling or something, or maybe crouching to spring.

I guess the place even got to Kathy, since she didn't put up much of a fight when I suggested we stick together instead of separating so we could look through the place faster.

But as it turned out, we were pretty lucky. We'd only been there for fifteen or twenty minutes when we spotted something. Way back in one corner, the one farthest from the gate, was a single line of cars, mostly without tires, some without hoods, and almost all without headlights. And at one end was not one rusty Edsel, but two. Like the suits, you couldn't tell them apart. Both had four missing tires, both had the same crumpled bumper, the same bashed-in trunk, and the same busted windshield.

This was a *spaceship?*

"Come on," Kathy said. "Where's the watchamacallit he gave us?"

Shaking a little, I reached into my pocket and took it out.

I took a couple of steps closer to the twin Edsels. And sure enough, a little glowing spot appeared on the side window of one of them, like a night light.

If it hadn't been for Kathy, I probably would've stood there staring half the night, but she grabbed the card out of my hand and ran up to the two cars. But even she hesitated just a little, maybe two or three seconds, like she had before she stuck her finger into the rock back in the ravine.

Then she touched the glowing spot with the card.

And the whole side of the car just melted away. Vanished, just like that.

· 14 ·

"I Don't See Any Seatbelts in this Thing."

E xcept for the missing side, the rest of the outside still looked like a rusty Edsel without wheels, just like the real one beside it. But what we could see of the inside was something else. It made the imaginary rock look like small potatoes.

For starters it was filled with a soft, blue light. It was also lots bigger on the inside than the outside. It was sort of like Dr. Who's TARDIS, where he got roughly two cubic miles of space inside that blue phone booth of his.

I just stood there with my mouth hanging open, but Kathy, being Kathy, jumped inside almost the second the wall disappeared.

"Come on," she said, which was getting to be her

favorite saying lately. "What are you waiting for, an invitation?"

I wasn't waiting. I was paralyzed. Probably with common sense. I'd been *yanked* into the rock, but here I had to climb in by myself.

"Come on!" Kathy repeated, and I guess the sight of her standing safely inside and waving her arms at me like an anxious third-base coach unfroze me enough to jump in after her. Or climb in, anyway. I still wasn't up to jumping.

With all the extra space that couldn't really be there, we had plenty of room to stand up straight, or play basketball if we'd had a hoop. In fact, we couldn't touch the ceiling even if we stood on each other's shoulders. The ex-*suit* probably couldn't even reach it. The place was at least ten or twelve feet square and more than that high, quite a bit more. Besides us, the only thing in the ship was what looked like a huge armchair sitting in front of a counter at one end. I figured the chair must be facing "front," even if it was at the back end of the "car."

While I was looking around and sort of waiting for the roof to fall in or for me to wake up and realize that the whole thing was just the result of one too many chocolate-flavored pepperoni pizzas at Bjornsen's, Kathy took the plastic watchamacallit and touched it to a glowing spot by the door.

And of course the door closed. Or the opening vanished, I guess is what I should say. Nothing really moved. The wall just sort of appeared, like things appear out of nowhere in a movie, only this was real, not special effects.

We went to the chair then. It was really huge. The seat was level with our chests, and the counter it faced was over our heads.

We scrambled up, and the seat sort of grabbed at us, like Velcro or whatever they call that stuff that sticks to itself, but it didn't hang on hard enough to keep us from moving if we wanted to.

On the counter a couple inches in from the edge was another glowing spot. This one was green. The ones by the door had been blue.

Then Kathy was standing next to me, the plastic thing still in her hand. This time, though, even *she* held back for a couple seconds.

But that was all, just a couple seconds.

She touched the card to the green spot, and a pair of black handles at least two inches thick popped out of the white countertop like a couple of jack-in-the-boxes. There were finger grooves in them, like in a video game joystick, but there were too many of them—six, not counting the one for the thumb—and they were too big. For us, that is. For the ex-suit, they would've been just right, like everything else in here.

"They *look* simple enough," Kathy said.

"They also look pretty far apart," I said. By leaning forward and stretching my arms as far as they'd go to each side, I could reach them both, but just barely. And I'd never be able to move them, if that's what we were supposed to do.

"We can each take one," Kathy said, nudging me to one side.

So we did. We still had trouble reaching them, and we

finally ended up standing in the seat and halfway sitting on the armrests and resting our elbows on the counter itself. And of course we had to use both hands to hold on to the controls. It wasn't very comfortable, to say the least.

"So," Kathy said after a minute or so, "maybe we better turn it on."

"You've still got the watchamacallit."

And we both stared at the glowing spot for a while. My stomach was twitching, and I bet Kathy's was, too. I'd never seen her hesitate anywhere near this long, for *anything*.

But finally she touched the watchamacallit to the spot again.

Something hummed, and that was all the warning we got. Then the whole ship vanished except for the controls and a little section of the counter around them. Even the "chair" vanished, but we could still feel it under us. It— and everything else—was just transparent, like glass, only more so, and we could see out in all directions, even up and down. I hoped it didn't look the same way from the outside.

"You ready?" Kathy asked.

"Ready?"

"To find out how these things work!" She was starting to sound impatient again, or maybe she was just nervous, like me.

"Sure I'm ready," I said. As ready as I'll ever be, I thought, which wasn't all that ready. "I don't see any seatbelts in this thing, so we better take it slow."

She gave me a "do-I-look-like-an-idiot?" look and then

wrapped her fingers around the control stick on her side of the counter. She tilted it back a smidgin, and I saw right away why there weren't any seatbelts—unless that Velcro stuff *was* a seatbelt.

Anyway, we didn't need any, because it wasn't the ship that moved. Everything else moved. Everything outside, that is.

At least that's what it looked like. Artificial gravity, I suppose. What really must have happened was, the ship tilted backward so its nose was pointed up in the air twenty or thirty degrees. But it looked—and *felt!*—like we were still perfectly level and the whole world had shifted around us, so that now we were on the side of a steep hill, with all the junk looking like it was getting ready to roll all over us.

I shut my eyes for a second, and when I opened them, I saw a little circle of reddish light hanging in the air in front of me. It looked like a gun sight, and I guess that's what it was, sort of, only it wasn't for aiming a gun. It was for aiming the ship. When I moved sideways to try to look around it, it moved with me. It just stayed right there in front of my eyes and it always pointed at the same thing outside, which right then happened to be the antenna of a junked Chevy a few yards away.

Then Kathy started fiddling with the controls again, and my stomach tried to climb out through my ears when all of a sudden we weren't just on the side of a hill but— Well, it looked like the world had been turned completely upside down. I mean, we were standing there and the whole world—or Harry's Junkyard, anyway—was hanging in the air over our heads, looking like it was going to drop on us any second. And under our feet was *nothing*. Except for open sky, that is, and stars. And the moon off to one side.

But eventually Kathy got the world right side up again, and we were pointing along an aisle toward a fence.

"Your turn," she said. "Your stick must be the speed control."

I swallowed hard and pulled at my control as lightly as I could.

Nothing happened.

I pulled a little harder, and it moved. It didn't tilt like Kathy's did. It just moved back toward me through the visible part of the counter, like a periscope through milk.

"You're backing up!" Kathy yelled, and I suddenly realized that the fence in front of me was moving away.

I pushed the control away from me. Too far, of course. We almost hit the fence before I pulled it back. What made it so hard was that I couldn't *feel* the ship moving. Besides, it was pretty dark, even with the moon and those three or four lights of Harry's.

Or maybe I was just being my usual, klutzy self.

Anyway, after a dozen bounces back and forth, I got the control back in neutral. I also realized there was a little sticking point—"detent," Dad would call it—right in the middle, so you could be sure you had the thing at zero. Even so, it wasn't that easy to find. I wished there were some kind of marks, like "miles per hour" or something like that.

And that's when I saw the little squiggles hanging in midair just under the "sighting circle." It was like the ship had heard me thinking, and maybe it had. If it could have all this space inside and still look like a rusty car on the outside, it could probably do *anything*. But even if the squiggles were some sort of speedometer, the units were probably something like Geezenstacks per wartlefarb, which wouldn't be a lot of help to someone who can't even convert things to metric.

While I thought about wartlefarbs, Kathy tilted the ship again. This time she pointed it up over the top of the fence around the junkyard.

"Ready to start moving?" she asked. *She* obviously was.

I swallowed again, but it didn't do a thing for my twitchy stomach, especially when I thought about the ex-suit waiting for us back in the ravine while whatever it was he breathed ran out.

I nodded to Kathy and nudged my control forward.

We were over the fence in a second, with nothing but sky in front of us. I of course panicked instantly, and my head filled with visions of us zipping right out of the atmosphere before we could stop. I jerked the control back, missing the zero point three or four times in each direction.

When I finally got us stopped, Kathy was looking at me like I was totally hopeless, which is about the way I felt. I'd felt the same way when I learned to ride a bicycle. I'd watched everybody else do it, so I knew exactly what I was *supposed* to do, but knowing and doing don't have much to do with each other, at least for me. Even with the help of a little hill to coast down, I spent a day and a half falling over before I finally got the hang of it. It took another two days to get my feet and hands working together so I could pedal and steer at the same time, which was sort of essential if I ever wanted to go anywhere that wasn't downhill.

Anyway, Kathy finally quit looking at me and started nudging her control until we were pointing down again. I nudged mine until we were three or four feet above the street about half a block from the junkyard fence.

And that, of course, is when a sheriff's patrol car showed up.

It was going through the intersection a couple hundred yards in front of us, crossing the street we were hovering over. The driver must've seen us out of the corner of his eye, because all of a sudden tires were squealing and the patrol car was lurching to a stop and backing up and then roaring toward us like something out of a TV cop show.

Neither of us had any idea how we looked from the outside, so for all we knew, we might look like something the driver would sooner shoot than look at, particularly if the driver was Pippenger. More important, we didn't know if this thing was bulletproof. We both knew that Wonder Woman's glass airplane was, but that didn't really prove anything except that we'd both read too many comic books.

So this time we both panicked, though Kathy at least waited until the deputy—it wasn't Pippenger—got out of the car and actually reached for his gun.

She jerked back on the control and the whole world tilted again. I shoved mine forward and then twisted around to look back, which was pretty much straight down now.

It was like one of those movies they used to take with a camera strapped to a rocket when it took off, only more

120

so. The ground was shrinking like crazy. The street lights were zipping together like they were being yanked in by giant rubber bands. I couldn't even *find* the lights of the patrol car.

Then everything started swinging around again. Kathy was twiddling her control again. I managed to get mine back in its neutral notch after only a couple of over-shoots.

Kathy and I looked at each other. We were both breathing hard and shaking. Her eyes were pretty wide, but probably not as wide as mine.

"Well," she said in a shaky voice, "that takes care of that idea."

"What idea?"

"I thought maybe we could take this thing out for a ride once we got the suit in here so he could breathe again. You know, to Mars or Chicago or someplace like that. But I guess we better not. Unless he wants to take us."

It was the first time I'd ever heard her actually admit there was something she was afraid to try. So I didn't argue while she slowly tilted the invisible ship until it was pointed down again. All the lights of East Gradwohl—at least I *hoped* it was East Gradwohl—were down there, squished together till the whole thing looked like it was only a few inches across. We must've been five or six miles up, at least.

Very slowly, starting and stopping and backing up at least a dozen times, we got back to the ground. We came down in a field a couple miles east of town, way out past the bypass. A dozen cows stood around ignoring us, or maybe sleeping. There was enough moonlight for us to see a farmhouse and a barn and other odds and ends a quarter of a mile away.

"I think," I said, "we better practice a little."

"Do we have time?"

"We've still got a couple hours till he runs out of air. And if we *don't* practice, we'll be lucky to get this thing into the park, let alone down in that ravine. We won't do him any good if we wreck his ship before we can pick him up."

She agreed, but she wasn't any too happy about it, and neither was I. We both knew how long it took me to get the hang of something.

For over half an hour, we practiced. We even took time for Kathy to jump out and see what we looked like from the outside, which turned out to be the same old rusty Edsel. We still weren't very good, unless you compared us to how bad we were at the start. The big problem was that we each had our own control. It was like trying to ride a bike while one person pedaled and the other one steered and neither one had any idea which way the other one wanted to go. We came to a lot of very sudden stops, for one thing. Except for one haystack, though, we didn't actually hit anything, which seemed like a miracle, considering the way we blundered around. We even tried switching controls once, but that was even worse.

Finally, we were ready. Or as ready as we figured we had time to get. With the ex-suit scheduled to run out of air—or whatever it was he breathed—in a couple of hours, we'd just have to do the best we could.

The best way to get to the park, we decided, would be

to go straight up a couple thousand feet, far enough to be out of sight of the ground but not high enough to run into any jet liners. Then we'd set ourselves up right over the ravine and go straight down. Provided we could see the ravine at night, that is.

It was a nice plan, and it would've worked just fine except for one small detail, which we discovered when we got over the park and looked down. All four of the sheriff's patrol cars were parked alongside the ravine, two on each side.

And their spotlights were all pointing down into the ravine, right at the "rock."

15

"He's Sure He's Going to Make the Network News."

Very carefully, we went down to maybe four hundred feet. At that height, we could see that there was more than lights pointed at the ex-suit and his imaginary rock. There were also a few guns, and one of them, some kind of high-powered rifle, was being held by Sheriff Pippenger.

Nobody was saying anything, as far as we could tell from that far up. It looked sort of like some movie I'd seen on TV last summer, where this spaceship landed and the National Guard and everyone came running and lined up around it and pointed guns and cannons and things at it. Only the spaceship had been able to defend itself—it melted a couple of the cannons, I think—but the ex-suit was probably having trouble breathing by now, let alone melting cannons.

And we still didn't have any idea if this thing we were in was bulletproof. Besides, if we tried coming down, Pippenger or someone would let loose, and the ex-suit very definitely was *not* bulletproof.

We were still trying to think of something we could do— besides give up, that is—when that same loose-wire voice started coming from somewhere. We couldn't understand what it was saying, it was so faint, and we couldn't locate it, either. It was like it was coming out of the air all around us, so we couldn't put our ears next to it to hear better.

But finally, by holding our breaths, we were able to make out something.

"Come closer," it said. That's all. "Come closer," over and over and over.

We looked down at the cars and the guns and decided we could take a chance on going down a *little*. No one was looking up, at least not yet.

We stopped again a couple hundred feet up and held our breath some more.

"Can you hear me?" I asked the air. "Or is this just one way?"

The "Come closer"s stopped.

"Yes," the voice said, "I can hear you." It was still as full of holes as the last time, but we could make it out, more or less.

"Is this a radio of some kind?" I asked, which should give you some idea of how well my brain was working right then.

Kathy made a face and said something like, "No, it's a chocolate-chip cookie," but then the ex-suit's loose-wire voice started up again.

"I do not have much time," it said.

"Your air is running out?" I asked.

"Yes. I am already becoming weaker. I fear that in another hour, it will be too late."

There wasn't any emotion in the loose-wire voice that his translating gadget was putting out, but I could imagine what he felt like. I felt almost as bad myself. We should've just gone ahead and tried to get him while it was still daylight, no matter what the problems. At least the place wouldn't have been surrounded by Pippenger and all those guns the way it was now.

"Is this thing we're in bulletproof?" I asked.

"Of course, if it is operating properly. It must resist many forces in space."

"Then if we could come down right next to you, you could jump in and you'd be okay." *If* we could get the ship next to him. *If* Pippenger didn't start blasting the second he saw the ship.

"It would take a great deal of time. I am unable to move very rapidly."

"Because of the air?"

"That is correct. I do not believe I can stand upright."

"Maybe we could help," I said. "If we got out of the ship down there, and showed ourselves, Pippenger *couldn't* shoot."

"Don't be too sure," Kathy said. "Besides, he'll probably *already* be shooting, before we ever get a chance to get out where he can see us."

For all I knew, she could be right. But still, I couldn't see anything else we could do. I mean, if we just *left* him there, he'd be dead in an hour or so anyway. But there had to be *some* way we could get down there and get him out without getting him—or us—shot full of holes!

If I'd had two or three days to think, maybe I'd've been able to come up with something, but I didn't.

Kathy, however, was another story. She doesn't need two or three days to think things up. Like with the black suits and the UFOs, things just pop into her head. There's no way she could come up with things like that logically, but she still comes up with them.

And that's what she did now.

"Come on, Calvin," she said, "let's get to my place, fast!"

"Your place?"

"Don't be an echo. Let's go!"

So we went. I didn't have any ideas myself yet, so I was ready to try whatever she'd come up with, even if she didn't want to take the time right then to tell me exactly what it was.

But while we were zipping across town, she explained, and I had to admit, it was a really neat idea. Remember that papier mâché boulder I mentioned before? The one she made for a school play last year and still has in her garage? Well, that's what we were going to her place to get.

And *then* we were going to get Deputy Hostetler to help us. Now *that* part of her plan is the sort of thing that I probably would've thought of myself. Eventually. I mean, the ex-suit's air was running out even faster than he'd thought it would, and he'd sounded like he didn't think he'd be able to get into the ship under his own power, so it was only logical to figure that we needed Hostetler's help. After all, who else besides Hostetler did we know who had even half a chance of being able to lift something that big? As for our own chances of being able to talk Hostetler into helping us—well, it didn't really make a lot of difference. We had to try. He was pretty much the only game in town.

Anyway, we zipped across town a couple hundred feet up and spotted Kathy's house in a minute or two. We were rushing, of course, but when we tried to come down, we were rushing just a little too much. But in a way, it was lucky we were, because that's when we found out a couple of things.

First, our half hour of practice hadn't done us—or me, anyway—as much good as we'd thought.

And second, it hadn't been skill or luck that had kept us from bumping into things. It was some kind of bumper built into the ship. On the way down, I didn't pull my control back to neutral fast enough, but the ship stopped anyway when its nose was an inch or so from Kathy's garage roof. And the control snapped back into neutral by itself.

Anyway, once we recovered, we felt a little safer, and we got the ship down off the roof and into the alley in a hurry. Kathy dissolved the side of the ship, jumped out, and ran into the garage through the side door. A few seconds later, the main door clanked up and she came running out carrying the boulder. She lowered the door behind her—loud enough for the whole neighborhood to hear, it sounded like—and tossed the boulder into the ship like a big, lumpy beach ball. As it clumped around and settled down, I saw there was a carrying strap made out of a half dozen pieces of string on the bottom. The whole thing, chicken-wire frame and all, couldn't weigh more than a pound. It wasn't *quite* as big as I remembered, but it was probably big enough, maybe four feet high instead of five. Up close, it didn't really look like a boulder, but I guessed that wouldn't really matter either.

Next came the hard part of her plan, talking to Hostetler.

We zipped back to the park, taking it faster than ever now that we knew about the built-in bumpers. We landed in the middle of a bunch of trees a couple hundred yards back from where all the commotion was. Lucky for us, Hostetler was on the park side of the ravine, so we could more or less sneak up on him through the trees once we got out of the ship. Unlucky for us, Pippenger was on the same side, practically next to him.

Kathy and I stopped maybe forty feet from them, where we still had some trees to hide behind. Pippenger was standing in front of one of the cars, right in the headlights, looking down into the ravine. Hostetler was a few feet away, shaking his head now and then.

While I was still trying to figure out some way of getting his attention, Kathy ran a dozen yards back to a path we'd just crossed and poked around on the ground. She was back in a few seconds with a handful of pebbles.

"Here," she said, dumping a bunch of them in my hand. "If you think you can throw them without beaning Pippenger."

I waited until Hostetler finally moved a few feet further away from Pippenger, maybe eight or ten, and then I let loose with the first pebble and ducked behind our tree.

The pebble landed twenty feet short and no one saw or heard it, except Kathy and me.

I threw the second. It was a little closer, but still nothing happened except that Kathy started making faces and acting like she was going to start throwing pebbles herself. Hostetler looked like he was getting ready to walk back toward Pippenger.

I threw a third pebble.

Bingo! It landed right at Hostetler's feet and went bouncing past.

I was already behind our tree, but when Hostetler turned around to look, I came out in the open again. I waved at him to come toward me. I could see him frowning and squinting against all the lights.

I tossed another pebble. This one fell short but bounced almost to his feet.

I moved a little closer, hoping no one else looked in my direction.

Finally, he saw me. For a second, he just looked disgusted, and I was afraid he was going to turn around and tell Pippenger, but he didn't. Instead, he took a quick look at the sheriff over his shoulder and walked slowly out of the glow of the headlights toward us. Then he moved faster, practically running. When he got closer, Kathy came out from behind the tree, too. He looked even madder when he saw her.

"What are you two kids doing out here?" he asked, but he asked it in a whisper. "Are you both crazy?"

"We've got to show you something!" Kathy said, and I sort of echoed her.

"You could get yourselves *shot*, sneaking around here like this!" he said. "Pip's convinced there's some kind of monster down there, inside that rock, and he's ready to blast anything that moves! He's even called the National Guard and—"

"There *is* a monster in the rock!" Kathy said. "Only it isn't really a monster, it's a tourist, and he—"

"Now hold on a minute!" Hostetler cut Kathy off. Then he turned toward me, still frowning. "Calvin, you've got a level head on your shoulders. Before I phone your folks and have them come and get you, maybe you can explain what's really going on. And what you two were *really* doing down in that ravine for half the afternoon."

All of a sudden I almost relaxed. For the first time in the last ten hours, I could tell the truth, which is probably what I *should* have done in the first place, when Hostetler spotted us coming out of the ravine.

So we moved back where Pippenger couldn't hear us, and I told him the whole story, as fast as I could.

"That's crazier than what Pip's been saying," he said when I finished. "*He* said he decided to take another look around down there, just in case you kids were cooking up another surprise for tomorrow, something that would get you another day off from school, and he tried to lean against that rock, only it turned out it wasn't a rock, and he fell in, right into the lap of this—this *monster*."

He shook his head. "He's *sure* he's going to make the network news tomorrow. He's already called every TV station in the state, and the National Guard. But so far there's nobody here but someone from the *Gazette*. After what happened this afternoon, I guess—"

"But it's true!" Kathy said. "There *is* a big hairy thing inside that rock down there, only it isn't really a rock. And if we don't get him back inside his ship right away, he'll die!"

"Just take a look at his ship!" I said. "You'll see!"

For maybe ten or fifteen seconds, he just stood there, looking like he was arguing with himself, but finally he sort of slumped, like he was relaxing.

"Okay," he said, "but if I didn't know your Dad, Calvin, and *you*— Come on, let's see this so-called 'ship.'"

And we ran, back through the trees and across a picnic area and into the next batch of trees where the ship sat waiting, hovering a foot off the ground, still looking like a rusty Edsel without wheels. Hostetler, puffing a little, frowned again when he saw it.

"Will *said* he ran into something like this," he said, "out by the junkyard."

"This is the ship!" I said, and then I ran up to it and touched the little blue glow with the triangular watchamacallit. Just like before, the side of the "car" disappeared, and we were looking at that ten-by-ten-foot, glowing room inside the six-by-four-foot passenger compartment.

Hostetler's jaw practically hit the ground, almost like Mr. Ames when the suit suddenly became the ex-suit, and he said a couple of things he normally didn't say around eleven-year-olds.

Kathy and I hopped inside and motioned for him to

follow. After a few seconds, he poked his head inside and looked around.

"This isn't possible," he said. "I don't care if I *am* seeing it, it just isn't possible."

"We know," I said, "but here it is anyway."

He got the rest of the way in then, practically an inch at a time. When he was all the way inside, I touched the spot that closed the door, and he jerked around and looked for a second like he was going to pound at the wall.

But he didn't. He just swallowed kind of loud and looked around again and then at us.

"Okay," he said, "you said you had something you wanted me to do?"

16

"Let Me Know if Your Hairy Friend Makes It."

So we told him how we wanted him to help us save the ex-suit.

He looked sort of thoughtful at first, but then he grinned just a little and nodded.

"To tell the truth," he said, "I've been thinking about telling Pip to stuff all his orders and just taking a walk down there to look at that rock for myself."

Then he grinned a little wider. "You know, if I play this right, I just might get my old job back from Pip this next election."

So we more or less synchronized our watches, and Hostetler got out and watched us while we took the Edsel back up to cruising altitude, which was only treetop level for a short hop like this.

Five minutes later, we'd told the ex-suit what was going to happen—what we *hoped* was going to happen and he said he would be ready, but he was sure he would need a lot of help to move very far. He had been sitting perfectly still and using as little of his air as he could, but he was sure he didn't have much longer to go. At least his translating gadget seemed to have recovered, so most of the holes were gone from his voice and he didn't have to repeat everything five or six times, which he probably wouldn't have had the strength to do anyway.

Then we were working the ship down through the trees and bushes as quietly as we could, until it was at the bottom of the ravine maybe a block and a half from the rock. Then, once we were down practically on the ground, we worked it forward. It made a little noise, but not a lot, and anyway, while we were doing this, Hostetler was supposed to be making a little noise of his own, talking to Pippenger.

Finally, we were as close as we dared get, maybe a hundred feet from the ex-suit and his rock. Any closer, and we'd start to get into the edge of all the light from the patrol cars' headlights.

Taking the papier mâché boulder, we jumped out and closed the door behind us so the blue light from inside wouldn't give us away. We got a little closer, maybe another twenty or thirty feet. We were just in the edge of the light, but we were under a really big tree that I was pretty sure nobody could see through.

And we waited.

We could hear Hostetler and Pippenger arguing, with Hostetler getting louder all the time.

Then Hostetler got *really* loud, so we could actually hear what he was saying, and I suppose everyone else could, too.

"Look, Pip, it's about time you got it through your head! The networks aren't coming! And neither's the Guard! And I don't blame them! I don't know what you think you're up to with this crazy story of yours, but—"

"Deputy!" Pippenger bellowed. "I will not stand for this open insubordination! If you can't control yourself, you can consider yourself unemployed!"

"We'll see who's unemployed when the election comes around! Right now, I'm going down there and take a look at your 'rock monster'!"

Then there were sounds of someone scrambling down into the ravine, loud sounds, and Pippenger was bellowing again.

"Hostetler! You get back up here! I will not have you endangering this entire community with your rash actions!"

But Hostetler didn't answer. Then we could see him at the bottom of the ravine, a few yards beyond the rock. He hesitated, like he was having second thoughts. He probably couldn't see us back in the shadows under the trees.

Then he started forward.

And Pippenger started down after him.

We've had it, I thought. Now we've really had it.

But Hostetler, instead of turning around to face Pippenger, ran the thirty feet or so to the rock. From what we'd seen when we'd been up above, the rock was visible from the edge of the ravine, but not really *very* visible. Even with all the lights, there were a lot of trees and things to block the view, which was part of what we'd been counting on.

Anyway, while Pippenger was still thrashing through the bushes and branches sliding down into the ravine, Hostetler was next to the rock. His face looked like he was getting ready to jump into a box full of spiders, but he didn't hesitate, even a second.

He leaned forward, right into the rock, and we could see him twitch for just a second, and then he was almost entirely inside the rock, with just his back showing outside. Since there weren't any yells or anything from up on the edges of the ravine, I guess nobody could see him well enough to see what he was doing for sure.

Anyway, he squatted down, with his back still the only part of him we could see, and then he stood up, slowly, and he looked like he was shaking a little, like he was really straining. Like the ex-suit wasn't able to stand up, even with help, and Hostetler was having to pick him up and carry him.

Then the rock was up off the ground.

And it was coming toward us. Since it was in front of Hostetler, we couldn't really see *him* at all. From the back, I suppose all you could see was his back sticking out of the rock.

About then, Pippenger hit the bottom of the ravine and started yelling at Hostetler again. And coming toward him.

The rock started toward us faster, sort of bobbling, like Hostetler was staggering, which he probably was. And no wonder, considering the size of the thing he was carrying.

Then he was with us, back in the shadows, practically

falling down. The ex-suit, still inside the rock, hit the ground with a thud, and Hostetler backed out of it, grabbed the papier mâché boulder from Kathy, and ran back into the light just as Pippenger reached the spot where the other rock had been. Pippenger had left his rifle or shotgun or whatever up at the top of the ravine, but he had his revolver out, pointing at Hostetler. We crouched as far back in the shadows as we could.

"Hostetler!" Pippenger said, squinting as he looked at the deputy. "How did you do that? How were you able to move that thing?" He kept the gun pointing right at Hostetler.

We could see Hostetler take a deep breath, and then he said, in the same loud voice he'd been using before, "It was easy, Pip! Here, catch!"

And he threw the boulder, sending it arching through the air in the open space between a couple of the trees, right at Pippenger.

For a second, I thought Pippenger was going to shoot the boulder, but instead he just ducked.

"You take care of that one," Hostetler said, still very loudly. "I'll check back here and see if it has any friends."

And then he was back in the shadows with us, behind some bushes, and we could hear the other deputies up above laughing. And there was a flash of light brighter than the headlights, and then more laughter. The guy from the *Gazette* taking a picture, I suppose.

"Where's the ship?" Hostetler was saying to us as he squatted down half inside the rock again. "And hurry up! This thing's about done for, whatever it is!"

Then he was struggling to stand up, obviously carrying

a heavy load, with only the back of his uniform visible outside the rock.

It seemed like it took an hour, but it was probably only thirty or forty seconds. Looking back over our shoulders as we led Hostetler to the ship, we could see Pippenger poking at the papier mâché boulder, then picking it up, and we could hear more laughter and a couple of cat-calls. Then Pippenger threw down the boulder and looked toward us, but it was pretty obvious he couldn't see us back in the shadows. And we were getting far enough into the trees and bushes that we could hardly see him.

But then he started after us. Or after Hostetler, since he didn't know we were back here.

"He's coming!" I whispered.

"Is the door open?" Hostetler asked between gasps for breath.

"I'll get it," I said, and ran ahead.

I waited until he was staggering right up to the side of the ship, and then I opened the door and hoped Pippenger was still too far back to get an eyeful of that blue light.

Then the rock was in the door, and something hit the floor with a thud, and Hostetler staggered back out, his face red, his whole body shaking from the strain.

Without a second's hesitation, though, he turned and headed back toward the approaching Pippenger.

"Now get out of here!" he said over his shoulder. "And let me know if your hairy friend makes it."

· 17 ·

"Who Knows *What* We
May Find. . .?"

And we got.

We maneuvered the ship back through the ravine maybe twenty yards, until we could see a clear spot overhead, where there weren't any tree branches or anything to get in our way. Then Kathy pointed it pretty much straight up, and I shoved the speed control all the way forward.

The ravine and the park just disappeared, and I yanked the control back into the center after only a couple of seconds.

And I looked back.

We were up lots further than the first time. A little speck of light down below was all that was left of East Gradwohl.

We didn't try to take it back down just then. Instead, we jumped back down to the invisible floor and started to look inside the rock.

But just as we were poking our heads inside, it disappeared.

The ex-suit, all ten hairy feet of him, was lying on the floor, sort of curled up, and for a second I thought he was dead and that the rock was fading out the way the hair fades off werewolves when they die in movies.

But then he moved. It was just a twitch at first, and then I could see that his hand was inside the hair around his waist, and it was doing something.

Then all of a sudden a pale pink glow filled the air around him, and he sucked in a breath that sounded like a really bad snore and looked like it could pull in all the air in the whole ship. For at least a minute, he just lay there, breathing like that.

Gradually, he got quieter, and then, slowly, he sat up.

And stood up. He was shaky, about like Hostetler had been after he'd carried him inside.

"Thank you," his translator said, and the words were full of holes again.

At which point, Kathy and I both gave big sighs of relief. "You're all right?" Kathy asked.

He did something that made the hair ripple all over his body, which maybe was his version of sighing with relief. "Yes," he said, "I will survive."

We were both quiet for a second, and then Kathy said, "You said your ship could show us where you're from."

Remember when I said it takes a lot to sidetrack Kathy?

"Oh, of course," the ex-suit said, as if he'd been expecting the question all along. He took the triangular watchamacallit from me and touched it to the counter. He moved it a little to one side. Then, all by itself, the ship moved.

When it stopped, the ground was straight ahead of us, the sky in back.

"Look through the circle," he said, pointing at the sighting circle still hanging in the air over the visible part of the counter.

We did.

And *everything* disappeared.

Not just the ship. The whole *world* was gone, and there was nothing in front of us but stars. Even *we* weren't there anymore. We were invisible, like the ship and everything else except the stars. The only thing we could see was the sighting circle.

And when we looked through it, there was nothing there. No star, nothing. There were stars all around it, but not in the circle.

"There's nothing there," the invisible Kathy said.

I felt something big and hairy nudge me to one side, and then the ex-suit's voice said, more or less, "Oh, dear. It must be too far away to show up. I am sorry. But that is the direction my world is in."

Then we were all visible again, and so was the rest of the world.

We tried asking more questions, but we'd already gotten all the answers he knew. He just didn't have any more, and besides, his voice was getting more and more full of holes all the time, and that bass gargle-yodel combination in the background was getting louder.

So he thanked us another dozen or so times and let us guide the ship pretty close to where we lived, and that was that.

When we got out and looked back at it, it didn't look like a rusty Edsel without wheels anymore. It looked sort of egg-shaped, although if you looked at it the wrong way, it could look like a saucer. It didn't glow or anything like that, and there weren't any windows, and it didn't make a single sound as it zipped up into the sky and disappeared.

I looked at my watch. It was almost midnight. Kathy just shrugged. "We'll think of something," she said.

"Maybe *you* will," I said. "Besides, I've got Walter to worry about."

But no matter what sort of trouble we ran into when we got home, I was glad we'd done what we'd done. I still had a sort of glow, knowing we'd actually saved the ex-suit's life. And if worse came to worse, we could always tell our folks the truth. Hostetler would back us up. I think.

And I still had the ring. And there was the Diefenbacher place to check out as soon as school was out. If it really *was* a place where the "tour buses" parked, like the ex-suit had thought . . .

And even if it wasn't, there was certainly *something* going on out there if one of the suits had actually bought the place. After all, that was the first place the ring—the "milorganite device"—had tried to lead me. And for a second there, when Mom had been turning the car around in the yard, I'd seen something through one of the windows. I think.

And then there was Walter. If he really did have some kind of talent for spotting aliens, that would be even better than the ring, since that thing only answers when one of them sends out a call. If Walter could spot them any old time he wanted . . .

I felt a tingle all over—not the kind I got from the ring—while Kathy and I made plans to bike out to the Diefenbacher place next Saturday. Or whenever our folks would let us out of the house again, anyway.

Who knows *what* we may find. . . ?